I0690608

The Two Straight Guys

First Edition

Published by The Nazca Plains Corporation
Las Vegas, Nevada
2009

ISBN: 978-1-935509-33-2

Published by

The Nazca Plains Corporation ®
4640 Paradise Rd, Suite 141
Las Vegas NV 89109-8000

PUBLISHER'S NOTE
The Two Straight Guys is a work of fiction created wholly by *Wade Wright*'s imagination. All characters are fictional and any resemblance to any persons living or deceased is purely by accident. No portion of this book reflects any real person or events.

Cover, Blake Stephens
Art Director, Blake Stephens

DEDICATION

To the multitudes of men that have found themselves in the same life struggling situation as Jim and Bill. To each of you, —past, —present and future, I salute each of you and wish each, and all of you, —the very best of happiness!

The Two Straight Guys

First Edition

Wade Wright

CONTENTS

CHAPTER ONE:

Bill First

"Well, hi Jim! What in the hell are you doing in here, at this time of day man?"

"Hi Bill! Can I kind of squeeze in here beside you?"

"Sure Jim! Things do seem to be kind of crowded in here today, but I guess we'll make it man. So, isn't this kind of a funny time of day for you to be here?"

"Yeah, it really is. I'm playing bachelor this week-end since Janice is at her annual accountant's convention in Boston, and so this is the week-end that we let Grandma and Grandpa Simmers have the kids for the week-end. Makes it easier for me, and they want to go for a week-end, anyway. So works out pretty well. What you doing here? I didn't figure I'd actually see anybody in here this time of day that I knew."

"Well Jim, I guess our week-ends are kind of similar then. I'm doing the ole bachelor thing too, this week-end. Sue is at the big interior design show in Philly, and of course I don't have the kid thing to worry about like you do."

"Yeah, you might not have the kid thing to worry about, but Sue is hanging out with all of those interior designers for the week-end! Now Jim, don't you really think that maybe you should have gone to that show with her to make sure one of those guys is not hitting up on her?"

"Oh, sure! Yeah, —right man!" Bill laughed back. "I'm really, really worried about those guys! Yeah, —right!" Bill again laughed back to Jim.

It was about 5:30 PM on a Friday afternoon, and Bill and Jim had happened to unexpectedly run into each other at, Jack's Cafe & Bar, a neighborhood lunch place and bar. A rather crowded, and kind of a cramped bar, on this afternoon.

The two men lived about two or three blocks from each other in a nice middle class neighborhood, and over the last few years they have had the opportunity to happen to see or talk to each other for a variety of reasons.

At one time they found themselves both on the same neighborhood improvement committee for the city, once each was invited to be part of a golfing foursome, and discovered, as they arrived, who the additional person was, and of course had run into each other at one or more of the local stores and filling stations.

Jim was about 32 or 33 years old, in good masculine shape, Janice, the accountant, was his wife and they had two children, a daughter, Janie, aged 13, and a son Bob, aged 10.

Bill was a couple of years older, his wife, Sue, was an interior designer and they, so far, have never had any children.

Bill was in construction, home construction, and Jim was a department store manager.

"Man, I don't think I've ever been in here when this place is so crowded before. This place is really packed today, isn't it?" Bill asked of Jim.

"Yeah, I will admit that since I never get in here at this time of day, I really did not realize this place was quite so popular. Friday afternoon at, — what, — 5:30? Why aren't all of these people home feeding the kids or something?" Jim asked in reply.

"Well Jim, maybe we are in the process of re-living the ole single life here for a few minutes. You know Jim, us ole married guys just don't get out into the living world, very often. Excuse me, sorry, did not mean to bump you, guy!"

"Hey don't worry about that. They have these bar stools so close together I think it's kind of impossible to not be bumping into each other." Bill said. "I think they have more stools along here than normal, don't they?"

Then looking around the room a little, Bill added, "Oh I see what the problem is. That group down there on the end, has moved two of those stools over from the other wall counter. So everything is all cramped up, all together. So anyway, I'm not trying to get fresh with you when I keep hitting your leg, OK?"

"You know what Bill? There just might be a very specific reason that group did move those stools. The way it would look to somebody, that was watching, would think for sure that you and I were trying to hit up on each other, with the way our legs keep hitting each other. And I'm sure, those guys down there on the end are taking very good advantage of the crowded conditions to play "leggys" with the gals."

"Yeah, probably right! Probably so!"

Bill and Jim continued to have their very uncommitted conversation about really nothing in particular, but were each enjoying the time of just being out with somebody interesting to chat with.

The bartender approached and asked. "Hey, another beer guys?"

Bill looked at Jim and asked, "You got time enough to have another?"

"Yeah, —yeah, I sure do. Like about all weekend, I think!" Jim laughed.

"OK, we'll each have another." Bill told the bartender.

"I'll buy these Jim. I think it might be better if only one of us tried to get to our billfolds. If we both reached back, —with the way we are packed in here, —it's hard telling just who's pocket we might be grabbing a billfold out of!"

"Well, I do admit that could be a problem. And you know what Bill? From watching all of the activity happening down there on the end of the bar, and with your leg rubbing up against mine, just trying to sit here, is starting to get some of my younger blood juices flowing. So, if I get acting kind of weird, just slap me back in place, OK?" He laughed as he looked at Bill.

"Hey, will do, but I sure can agree with what you said. I never get myself caught in a place with a lot of touching activity happening in front of me like it is down there, and yeah, I admit that I feel like my younger blood juices, as you put it, are flowing too."

Jim and Bill continued to sit there and slowly sip on their beers, and Bill every once in awhile noticed what he truly did think, was a little more leg contact than what had been happening earlier. He kept a good observation of Jim to see if maybe Jim was drinking a little more beer than maybe he should be. Bill decided a number of times that Jim was doing just fine. He was not acting funny at all, his speech was fine, and all of his actions were completely in line, well, —with maybe the exception of the more frequent leg contact. Bill did notice the additional contact, but he did not have a problem with it.

As they continued to have their conversation, Jim frequently would mention to Bill some activity that he had observed down at the end of the bar. He'd ask Bill to, "turn and look."

Finally Jim did say. "You know what man? I'm going to need to get out of here pretty soon. Janice is out of town till Monday afternoon, and all of this touching that is going on in front of me is starting to get me really horny and I'm not sure I have that much control, for that long!"

Bill looked down, and saw Jim rubbing his growing crotch.

Bill said. "Jim, you are not helping yourself by doing that! You are making yourself more excited!"

As Jim started to answer, he looked down at Bill's hand action and said, "Well, Mr. Bill, you're not helping yourself any either, and don't do that in front of me!"

Jim then leaned over closer to Bill and quietly asked. "Do you know of any place where I can get some sex? Do you know of any sex clubs around here?"

Bill rather shockingly replied. "No Jim, I really don't! I've never needed to find out. And I would guess you have never needed to either, since you are asking where they are. Right?"

"Yeah, right Bill. I should not have asked. Forget it!"

"No Jim. I think we are both in the same situation, and I don't think it is going to go away right away, even if we do just get the hell out of here. Jim, you had the guts to ask me something, now can I ask you something?"

"Yeah, —yeah, of course you can. What?"

Bill leaned over very closely toward Jim and asked. "Jim, have you ever wondered what it feels like to touch another guy?"

Jim rather flipped his head quickly toward Bill and kind of answered, "Well, —uh, —uh, —yeah. I have kind of wondered once in awhile in the past, but have never done any of that kind of stuff. Why are you asking me that?"

Bill then replied. "Well Jim, I have always wondered just what doing something like that might be like, and I've never had a chance to, and the way both of us are feeling, I was kind of hoping that maybe you might let me feel you and your body as you jack off? Could we maybe do that?"

Jim looked at Bill and just kind of sat there. He looked at Bill squarely in the face, —and did not say anything!

Bill then said, "Jim, —Jim, —I'm sorry I said that! Forget it man! I'm sorry!"

Jim then said. "Finish your beer. Let's go outside."

Bill grabbed his beer and gulped the entire bottom half of the beer.

Each man sat his beer mug down, waved at the bartender, and told him, "Thanks man. We'll see you later!"

They left the bar.

As they left the bar, they headed toward Bill's car.

Bill leaned on the trunk lid of his car and turned to Jim. "Jim, really maybe I should not have said that! God Jim! I'm really kind of sorry I ever said that. I'm not a gay guy. I've just never had a chance to do something like that and since I know both of us are horny, but don't have our women here, I just figured we'd probably just go home and jerk off, and then I thought maybe we could, but now, I think I was really stupid for saying that!"

"Well, Bill! I do admit that when you first said it, I was really shocked, but I very quickly lost the shock and immediately started to really kind of like the idea. Yeah, Bill, I'd love to have you feel me as I jerk off. I know most boys in school do that kind of stuff, but I never got to, and I missed out on that. Yeah, —hell yes man! I want to and am damn glad you had the balls to ask! So what do we do now?"

"Well, I guess go to my place. I mean, I guess. That's what we should do right? I mean, we don't need to go to a motel or anything like that, do we?"

"No, I don't think we need to do that! We'll just go to your place, and we'll just make sure none of the neighbors can see in any of the windows, so that what we do together is just between us, OK?"

Bill then said. "Yeah, yeah, —right. God man, now I am really getting feeling all funny. Jim, are you sure we should be doing this? I mean man, I've never ever grabbed some other guy. I know I was the one that suggested this first, but now I'm really feeling funny. Jim, we are both straight guys! Should we be touching each other like that, and especially while the other guy is jacking off?"

"Bill, I don't intend to write a newspaper article about it so that everybody in town knows about it. You and me! A private room! Some fun stuff that you and I both know millions of guys do all of the time, and for us, it will just happen to be something different!"

"Yeah, —millions of guys! Like the guys at the interior design convention. So, we think all of them are gay guys? Hey, if we are deciding to do something together, what makes us think that those gay guys might not decide to do something different, that they have never done before? Like some gal? Besides, Jim, some of those guys are damn nice looking and well built guys. Hell some of 'em are probably pretty well hung too! Gay or not, some of them are pretty good looking guys!"

"Bill, I have a funny feeling right now that you have looked at some of those guys in the past and wondered just what playing with them might be like, —haven't you?"

Bill looked up at Jim and very sheepishly said. "Uhhh —Jim,—yeah, I have. Yeah, I admit it. There have been times when I would look at two of them, and realize that those two guys make it together in the bedroom, and I've kind of wondered what it would be like to play with a man's body for a change. Yeah, —Jim, —yeah. I have kind of closed my eyes and tried to image it. Does that make me gay?"

"No, no— it does not make you gay! It just says you get horny once in awhile. Come on, let's get out of this parking lot."

The two men got in their respective cars and headed for Bill's house.

Bill used his automatic garage door opener, and then motioned for Jim to use the space inside beside his car.

They each parked their cars, and Bill closed the garage door.

Bill got out of his car and waited for Jim to come around the corner of the car. As he did, Jim reached out and took ahold of Bill's crotch.

Jim then said, as he slightly squeezed Bill's crotch, "Well this will be something different for us won't it? Sure as hell never imagined to be doing anything like this today, but I kind of figure it as, each day is for living, and doing whatever! Nervous, aren't you?"

Bill replied. "Yes, hell yes I am! Jim we are both married guys with wives. Are you really sure we should be doing this?"

"Bill, it's done everyday, everywhere! I'm nervous too. Look at me shaking. This is so weird for me, and I know it has to be for you too. Neither one of us expected our day to turn out this way, I know that for sure! For you, and me, it's just that neither one of us has done it before, so we will kind of need to help each other just kind of find out what to do. Bill, I guess it's just going to be try, —and see, —and do something different if it's not right. OK?

Bill said, "Yeah man, —but I'm scared kind of shitless right now! This is really just like the very first time you have sex with a girl. God I'm nervous!"

The men, the two very nervous but anxious men went into the house, through the kitchen/garage door.

As they went into the house, Bill turned to Jim and said, "Hey let's use the guest bedroom. I'd feel really funny using the bedroom that Janice and I use everyday."

Bill and Jim went into the guest bedroom. Looking kind of weirdly at each other, as if something very unexpected was going to happen to one of them, they watched each other get completely naked.

Jim looked at Bill and said. "Well, for me to have my first time in deciding if a man is hot and good looking and built nicely, I guess I have to admit I ended up with a pretty well taken care of guy."

Bill, looked at Jim, reached out his hand to place it on his chest and replied, "Well man. Thanks but I sure can not complain about my "playmate" if that is what I am to call you. For a guy that works in a store all day, you sure have kept your little boy body look, haven't you. I guess you must use the weight room a lot, uh? You've got a hell of a lot hotter body once you get all your clothes off, don't you? Shit Jim," Bill continued as he lowered his hand down toward Jim's waist, "You really are a hot looking man. You need to run around without a shirt on more often, I guess. Hey, you know I work with construction guys, and people always joke about how hot us construction guys are supposed to be, but shit man, —you sure have me beat all to hell!"

As Bill was exclaiming his pleasure of Jim's body built, Jim's manly dick was starting to get somewhat excited. Jim looked down at it, and commented, "Hey Bill, I'm certainly not used to having some other guy make nice comments about my naked body. I guess it is kind of getting me excited, isn't it?"

As Bill looked down to Jim's cock, even that action made it react more anxiously and jump as it did. Bill then said, "Hey Jim, I have never in my entire life ever commented about some other guy's body before, and to do that is making me feel kind of weird too."

"Bill, I'm not too sure of just how two guys start doing it with each other, but I will tell you though, that your hand on my skin is feeling really nice to me. So what if we went in and took a nice warm shower together, so that we will be kind of just standing there real close, and if we soap each other, then that will give us a reason to be touching each other, OK?"

"Yeah, yeah, that's an idea!" Bill answered.

The two men, now both carrying a stiff stick, which was bouncing up and down, they walked from the guest bedroom, went to the bathroom and both got into the shower. As Bill closed the shower door, Jim turned on the water and started to adjust it so that the temperature was just right.

Standing behind Jim, Bill placed both hands on Jim's waist. He then slowly moved his hands around to the front of Jim in such a fashion as to be hugging his waist.

Jim readjusted the temperature, and had his attention rather attracted toward that function as Bill slid his right hand down the side of Jim's body and placed it toward the front of Jim's right leg, immediately under his erect cock.

Jim threw his head up into the air and let out a moan. "Oh Bill, Oh my God Bill! Oh Bill I had no idea I'd feel like this! Oh God man! Put your other hand down on the other side, man!"

Bill then slid his left hand down, around to the front of Jim's leg and pulled himself up against Jim as he grabbed Jim's left leg, once again immediately beneath the now raging, bouncing, and throbbing hard-on, that Jim was supporting out in front of himself!

Bill's cock had gotten extremely hard as he reached his hands around Jim's body, and he had to flip it to a side, so that he could place his torso up against Jim's bare back side.

Bill pulled Jim back tighter and tighter to himself.

Jim moaned and dropping his head down, as if he had lost control of his neck muscles, and he again moaned, groaned and exclaimed, "Oh God Bill! Oh God Bill, grab my legs! Oh God Bill, let me feel your hands on my legs, man!"

The water was flowing over the two men as they did for the very first time, enjoy the feel of another man up against his bare body, and the ecstasy of having another fully grown man feeling his body, and being able to feel back.

As Bill was squeezing Jim's body and pulling it up to himself as completely as he could, Jim was reaching around with both of his hands, attempting to grab ahold of some part of Bill.

Suddenly Jim turned around so that he was face to face with Bill. He threw his hands around Bill's body and let each hand land firmly on Bill's butt cheeks. As he realized just where his hands had landed, he squeezed. "Oh man! I've got your butt in my hands Bill! I've got a hold of your bare butt, man!"

Bill had already reached around Jim's body, and he too had a hold of butt cheeks. "Yeah, I know man, yeah, I know, and I have your butt in my hands too! Oh God Jim! God Jim! Why in the hell didn't somebody tell me a hell of a lot earlier in life that feeling a man's body, felt so damned good!? Oh God Jim! Jim, I wish I had been doing this with some guy years ago! Oh Jim, you feel so good to me!"

Bill hugged Jim's body, and started to lower himself down somewhat so that he could put his face on Jim's chest. Jim realized what was happening, and loosened his grip just enough to let Bill slide down, but yet held on firmly enough so that Bill would not collapse completely to the floor. Jim had realized that Bill had lost all his leg strength, and his legs were getting very weak.

Bill moved down to the top of Jim's chest. He laid his head up against Jim's chest and slowly started to tongue the hair on Jim's chest. He moved it back and forth with his tongue! He sucked some of it into his mouth. He bit onto the hair that he had in his mouth and very slightly pulled on it.

Jim moaned, and lowly said, "Oh yes man. Oh my God Bill, nobody, and I do mean nobody, has ever done that! Oh God Bill, what a great feeling!"

Bill moved his head slightly lower and placed his face squarely in the middle of Jim's pecks. Bill buried his face as deeply into Jim's chest as he could. He pushed his face up against his chest so firmly that Jim had to quickly adjust his stance so that he did not get pushed over. Jim continued to moan with pleasure. He continued to hold Bill so that he would not collapse onto the floor, and continued to let him know verbally just how great this entire experience was turning out to be!

Bill moved his head to the right and took Jim's left tit into his mouth. All of a sudden, Jim was getting a tit sucking, and he let out an enormous moan of pleasure. "Oh my God Bill! Oh my God Bill! Oh God Bill, —I have never, —oh God Bill! Oh Bill, suck on that tit man! Oh shit man! Oh my God man! Oh God! Oh God, I had no idea that this could happen!"

"Oh my God Bill, you have to have been playing with other guys before right? Oh Bill, I'm not really your first guy, am I Bill? Oh my God Bill, —you've done this to other guys, —right?"

As Bill pulled his face back just slightly he said, "No Jim! No, I never have! Jim you are the first guy I have ever done anything like this with! Oh man! This feels so good to me too! Is everything alright with you man?"

"Oh shit Bill, nothing could be better man! Oh Bill! I am so damn glad you got the guts up enough to suggest we try this! Oh Bill! This is so much better than finding some slut gal and fucking her! Oh God Bill, I am so glad we are doing this. Oh chew on me man! Please!"

Bill had already replaced his mouth back onto Jim's tit and was biting on it so very gently and lovingly. As he did, Bill actually realized for the first time, that his actions on Jim's body were not just, "funny playing around", he realized as he chewed on Jim's left tit, that he was actually making love to Jim and to that tit! "This is not just playing!" Bill thought to himself. "I am actually making love to this man! I'm loving him and his body!"

That realization to Bill was not upsetting to him. When he realized it, he did have an instant of fear that he would completely reject, what he now knew he was feeling, but he did not. He accepted it as a very good, natural, happy and very pleasant experience.

Bill moved his face to Jim's right tit. Jim moaned as Bill placed the tit into his mouth. Jim grabbed ahold of Bill tighter and pulled him up closer to himself! "Oh Bill, chew my tit please! Oh please!" Jim moaned.

With their moving in the shower some, Bill was now getting a face full of water as he pressed himself up against Jim's furry chest, and chewed on his tight and firm tit.

Bill chewed on Jim's chest and his tits, then started to lower himself lower down on Jim's torso. His face landed in Jim's navel. Bill pushed his nose in the navel, and then licked it with his tongue! Jim continued to moan in very accepting and exciting manners.

Bill slid his tongue out, and slid his face down toward the top of Jim's fuzzy crotch. He placed some of Jim's fuzz in his mouth and pulled. He then went back to Jim's body and grabbed more. Jim moaned. He liked the feeling of having Bill pull on his crotch hair with his mouth.

Jim's stiff cock was right at Bill's face. Bill was hitting it with his face, and was rather playing with it by pushing it out of his way with the side of his face. He had not yet, put his mouth on it, but he was moving it and rather playing with it with his cheeks, and his chin. He was having fun with it, that when he would push it down, it would fly back up and hit his face.

The way Bill was playing with Jim's meat stick, made Jim get more and more excited. He realized that Bill had not yet actually touched it with either his hands or his mouth, but just the idea that some guy had his face down there and was pushing it around with the side of his face or using his chin on it, was something that Jim had never thought could ever happen. Every time, when it flipped back up from being pushed down, that made Jim more and more excited about what was happening to him.

Bill buried his face in Jim's crotch hair, and very slowly let his tongue out just a little so that he could feel the fuzzy hair on the tip of his tongue. He did not know if Jim could tell that he had done that or not. In one way, he rather wanted to have Jim know that he had, kind of, attempted to touch his dick and his bag with his tongue, but then at the same time, he was not completely sure that he wanted Jim to know just yet that he had done that. He was not sure just how Jim would react. They were supposed to be only playing with each other as the other guy jerked off. They had not even discussed anything like licking on the other guy. It wasn't going to go that far! What Bill had already done, while just there in the shower, was way beyond what they had talked about doing. Bill realized that they were both getting very, very excited about this activity! Much more, than they were supposed to, or had expected to. Bill had not expected to get so anxious and so sexually excited. He knew that Jim was a man, and he knew that he was not supposed to get excited about being with a guy!

As Bill pushed his face forward, he heard Jim say, "Hey my man, stand up here, please! You've got me so damned hot, I need to get my face up against you, now! It's my turn to find out what that feels like. Here Bill, stand up, please! Let me lick on you some! Bill I've got to see if doing it, feels as good as getting it done to you! Bill, let me at you, please!"

14

CHAPTER TWO:

Then Jim

Bill stood up and grabbed Jim around the waist and gave him a very mighty hug. He buried his face in the side of Jim's neck and slightly licked his neck before he pulled away.

Jim returned the emotion of laying his face against Bill's neck as Bill had just done to him. He returned the squeeze and slowly started to lower himself down the length of Bill's torso.

As he so slowly moved down Bill's body, he extended his tongue and so very lovingly licked Bill's chest, down the center line of his stomach and ended his journey right at the crotch bush, that Bill was presenting to him. He buried his face into Bill's fuzz and slowly moved it back and forth.

As Jim forced his face into Bill's fuzzy crotch, he did as Bill had done earlier to his cock. He pushed it from side to side with the side of his face.

He placed his chin on the top of Bill's hard-on rod, and forced it down, and then let it flip back up after he had pushed it down as far as he could push it. As it flew up, it would hit Jim in the face, and Jim would then slap his face against it to make it move sideways, only to come right back at him, and once against slap him in the face. Again, Jim would place his chin on it, as it stood erect and pointing directly at him, and again force it down as far as he could manager to get it to go.

As Jim pushed Bill's cock down, Bill would say each time Jim forced it, "Oh man! Oh man! Oh God what a feeling man! Oh Jim! For God's sake, why haven't we been doing this earlier? Oh Jim you feel so damn good to me down there!"

Jim's hands moved up and down on Bill's legs, and each time that they reached up, he grabbed Bill's butt muscles and squeezed. As he squeezed, he pressed his face tightly, into Bill's crotch!

Jim slowly started to stand up again, and as he did, he once again caressed the length of Bill's body, and as he reached Bill's chest, he leaned to his left and placed his mouth on Bill's right tit.

Bill softly said, "Oh Jim, lick it please! Oh please! Oh Jim, please put it in your mouth and suck on it, please!"

Bill wrapped his arms around Jim's body as he pulled Jim in closer to his tit, so that Jim could place it in his mouth and lick and suck on it.

"Oh yeah, man! Oh yeah, Jim! Oh God Jim! Oh my God Jim! I've never felt anything like this before! Oh Lordy Jim! Please do the other one man! Oh yeah, Jim! Oh Jim! My gosh, I've never, ever, felt anything like that before! Oh Jim, chew on it man! Kind of bite my tit man! Oh Jim that is making my dick so damn hard! Oh Jim I can feel them being connected. Jim I feel like my dick and my tits are connected when you do that! Oh shit man! Oh God! Ohhhh, —Jim! Oh man! You feel so good to me!"

Jim wrapped his arms tightly around Bill's torso and hugged and squeezed him very, very tightly!

Jim moved from tit to tit, back and forth chewing, licking and sucking on each tit, as he pinched the other tit with his hand. As he pinched, or as he chewed slightly, he could feel Bill loose his strength and rather slump as he moaned and groaned with the pleasure that he was finally experiencing for the first time in his life.

"Oh Jim! Oh Jim, for God sake man, —do me! Oh yeah! Oh yeah, do that some more man! Oh Jim, I love this, man! Oh Jim! Never, never did I ever think, until right now, that I would ever say that I wanted some man to play with any part of my body, but now man, you can use any part of me that you want! Oh God Jim! Oh shit man, I never ever thought I'd ever feel anything like this! Oh Jim, do stuff to me! I love feeling you up against me. Oh Jim, I did not know it, but man I love being played with by you. Oh Jim! I never thought I'd want some guy's hands on me, but Jim, —I'm yours to do with and play with! Oh shit man, I'm begging! Jim I know I'm begging, but Jim, I want you to do stuff to me and to my body. Please Jim, will you do it? Jim I know my begging is really kind of weird and a guy like me is not supposed to want it from another guy, but my God Jim, I am so damn horny for you right now! Jim, I want to say I love you! Can I say that, man?"

"Yeah, Bill, you can say that if that is the way you are feeling right now. I have to admit that I pretty well have those same feelings too, so don't be afraid to just tell me whatever you need to tell me."

"Bill, I know this is kind of weird for the two of us, but Bill something must be pretty natural about it or the two of us, so called, straight guys, would not be getting so excited about feeling and playing with each other like this! Bill, right now, I know why some guys are gay. Bill, right now, I am really wondering if maybe I am really a gay guy. Bill, to really be a straight guy, and then feel this way, when I've never even felt like this with my wife, Bill,

I think that is telling me something! Oh Bill, grab my butt man! Please! I want to feel your hands and fingers back there man!"

Bill did as Jim asked. He took ahold of each butt cheek with a firm and strong hand. He squeezed as he pulled Jim toward himself.

"Oh Bill!" Jim said. "Oh Bill, put your fingers up by my asshole, man! Bill I want to feel your hand up between my ass cheeks!"

Bill pulled Jim's butt cheeks apart and slid each hand toward the hungry asshole that Jim was wanting to feel Bill's hands explore and grope.

"Oh yeah, Bill! Oh Bill! Put a finger up in my ass, — please! Please! Bill I wanna know you have a finger up inside of me! Oh Bill! Please fuck my asshole with a finger man!"

Bill continued to pull and hug Jim up close to him, he laid his face across the manly chest that Jim possessed, and he reached around to the asshole, of his new found playmate, and perhaps, somewhat lover, —from the sounds of the interchange. He placed one middle finger up into Jim's tight, little asshole.

With Jim's asshole clamping itself tightly closed to prevent any alien entry, Jim needed to force his finger up and into the hole.

"Oh! Oh my God man!" Jim exclaimed as he felt Bill intrude into his inner side. "Oh God, Bill! Oh, —Bill I have got to do this to you, too! Bill —please let me finger your ass too! Bill you have no idea of what in the hell it feels like to have some guy's finger up in your ass! Oh Bill, please, please tell me I can put my finger up in you too! Please man! Please!"

"Yeah man! Oh, yeah! You can finger my hole man!" Bill replied. "Yeah if it feels that damn good to you, then let me have a feel too! Put a finger up in my ass man!"

Jim reached around Bill and after spreading his ass cheeks some, he inserted a finger up in Bill's ass as far as he could. He pushed it in, and then he moved it back and forth and around in a circle.

"Bill, —Bill how does that feel man? Bill, like that?"

"Oh shit man!" Bill said. Oh my God Jim! If just a finger feels like that up in there, for God sake, what in the hell does it feel like to have a dick pushed up in there, man? Oh my God man! Can you just imagine what in the hell it must feel like to get some guy's dick up inside of you if just a finger feels that damn good?"

"Bill, I really don't know, but Bill you have got me so damned hot and so damn horny, I want to find out! Bill I want you to fuck my ass with your dick, man! Bill, will you try to get your dick up in me? Oh shit man! Bill, —for God sake Bill, I can not believe that I am asking some guy to put his dick up in my ass man! Bill, is this meaning I'm really a gay guy? Bill, wanting to get my ass fucked by you, —does that mean I'm really gay and never knew it?"

"No Jim, it does not mean that! We just happen to be doing some different kind of stuff tonight that neither one of us has ever done before! And both of us are so fucking hot, and we're wanting stuff done that we have never done before. No Jim! Getting my dick up in your ass does not mean you are gay. Turn around man, lean over and put your hands up on the wall! I've got one raging hard-on, and I'm gonna find someplace nice and warm for it to go into. Turn around man, give me your ass, —give me your ass!"

"Yeah, but Bill! Bill I know I will never be able to get that stick of yours up in my ass without some kind of grease or something, so that it'll slide up in my ass. Bill, just getting your finger up in there I almost needed something on it. Bill, have you got some kind of grease or lube or something around here that we can use on my ass?"

"I don't have any lube of any kind Jim, but yeah, —we do have butter and some cooking grease in the kitchen. I'll be right back man. Turn this shower off and keep your ass ready, because now that you've asked for it, I am for damn sure, going to get in it tonight! Before you mentioned it, I really had not thought about sticking you with it, but shit man, —now you are going to get it! I've never realized before that I wanted to fuck some guy's ass, but man you have me so damn hot, I will probably want to do anything that you ask! I'll be right back!"

Bill got out of the shower, grabbed a towel and headed for the kitchen.

Jim turned the shower off and regained his position of leaning, with both arms and hands extended, against the wall of the shower, with his ass kind of bent out for easy access. Bill re-entered the shower.

"Hey man. I got some cooking grease. That should work OK don't you think? I mean, I've always heard of the stories about the gay guys and using it, so I guess it must work OK, or I don't think we'd have heard that stuff, do you?"

"Yeah, I think it'll work, but make sure you get plenty up in my ass before you start pushing that rod of yours up in there."

Bill spread a good amount of grease on Jim's ass and then asked, "Hey man, think that is enough?"

"Hell, I don't know!" Jim replied. "I've never been ass fucked before! How in the hell am I supposed to know? Just take it good and slow at first, so I can make sure this is still something that I want to do. Once that damn dick of yours gets close to my asshole, I might change my mind. If it hurts, I might change my mind, really quickly!"

Bill wiped the excess grease off of his hand. He moved up close to Jim's ass, he took ahold of his own dick, he directed it toward Jim's asshole and slid it up between Jim's ass cheeks. Bill hugged Jim around the waist with his right hand, and guided his dick with his left hand. He found the hole.

"Yeah man! Yeah, slow now! Go slow! I've got to make sure I can take this! Go in me real slow, man, real slow!" Jim pleaded and begged!

"Yeah I will. Can you feel the tip of my dick?"

"Hell yes man, hell yes! Yeah, Bill I can! You've got it right at my asshole. Move toward me a little more but just be slow! Yeah man! Yeah, move toward me and keep your dick aimed right at my hole, right where it is now!"

Bill squeezed Jim's waist as he pulled himself up closer to Jim, and thrust his dick forward so that it would enter Jim's ass. It snapped in! Jim jerked and yelled, "Ouch! Oh man! Oh shit man! Oh God man! Oh Bill, don't move! Oh Bill! When you pushed it in me, it hurt! I guess maybe I was not quite ready for it. Just stand there for a moment! It doesn't hurt anymore, but let me just try and get used to having something stuck up in my ass."

Then Jim laughed and added, "Well man, I guess you can say you just took my male cherry, can't you?"

Bill grabbed ahold of Jim with both hands wrapped around his body and asked, "Hey, man! You OK? Are you alright?"

"Yeah, I'm OK now, but for a second there, it did hurt. But now it's feeling pretty good up in there. Push up against me a little more and let's see if I can take more of it."

Bill pulled Jim's body up against his own, and pushed his dick in a little more.

"Yeah Bill, that feels good! Bill, see if you can get more of it in me."

Bill, once again, pushed his rod up against Jim's ass and let more dick enter into Jim's body. Jim did not complain or say to stop, so Bill continued to push, and shortly he discovered that he had all of his dick up and in Jim's ass.

"Jim, my baby! You have got all of me up inside of you now! How is that feeling? Is it OK? You did not tell me to stop, so I kept pushing, and now it's all up in you. You OK? How does your ass feel?"

Slightly turning and twisting his head, partly holding it up and partly letting it lay against the shower wall, Jim moaned, "Oh shit man! Oh God Bill! Oh Bill, —once that initial pain passed, man, ever since then, this has been great! I can not believe I have your whole damn dick up inside of me! God man! All we were supposed to be doing in here together tonight was feeling each other, as we jacked off. Man, —oh man! Bill, we sure, in the hell, went way past the just jerking off stage, didn't we?"

"Yeah Jim, we sure as hell did man, but Jim I don't have one regret about it! Jim, I think we should have been doing this for a long time now! Sex with you, and fucking you is great! I'm really having myself one hell of a great time! I love what we are doing. This is so much more exciting than I ever thought sex could be! Man, this is it! Jim, this is what really being a man is! Doing sex, in a big strong, rough, manly way, and we really are enjoying each other!"

"Bill that damn big thing up in there feels good! Hey, —kind of move it around some. Kind of jerk it back and forth and let me feel it. Oh Bill, I know already, I love to have a guy's dick up in my ass! Oh shit yes! Oh I thought having a finger up in there was great! Oh Bill! I've got to fuck your ass too, before we are done. Bill, you have got to see how damn good this feels! Oh shit man! I can not believe I am feeling so damn good having your cock up in my ass. Oh shit Bill! I never thought I'd ever say that I like having a man's dick up in my ass! But Bill, —I like having your cock up in my ass!"

Bill continued to hug Jim's mid torso, and started some serious fucking action, —back in his butt. He started slowly, and continued to listen for any instruction to stop or slow down or anything similar, but he never heard any. He decided that Jim's ass was feeling good, and he was anxious for this action. He started some serious fucking! Fast, deep and hard!"

"God Jim!" Bill said. "Jim, you're doing OK man? Is this OK with you? Are you feeling OK?"

"Oh yeah Bill! I am really OK! I am more than just OK! I am feeling damn good! Bill, I love this. Bill, I hope you will agree to do this to me often. Bill, you have got to get fucked too! There is no way to explain how great this feels! Oh man! Fuck me hard, please! Please fuck my ass, man! Fuck me! Fuck me! Fuck me!"

Jim was still leaning on the wall, letting his head hang down and swinging it back and forth in his almost unconscious state of being. He was living in a completely new and great new "world". He knew he was experiencing this, for only the very first time, of what he knew would be many, many times more in the future, and as often as possible.

As Jim was begging for Bill to fuck him, —fuck him hard, Bill said, "I really never had any interest in fucking some guy's ass before, but shit man, I think I just got converted over to being an ass fucker tonight! Shit man! I love this! Man do I love this! What a great feeling to be able to hang onto your big, strong, solid, body, and feel your muscles, as I fuck your asshole like crazy! I've never felt anything that good, that solid and that strong before. I really like being able to fuck you as hard as I can, and really grab ahold of you and your strong body while I do it to you! I kind of feel like I'm some wild animal, out in the wilds, fucking for all he is worth. And you're begging for more! Oh shit Jim! What else could a guy ask for?"

"Bill! Bill, let's lay down on the bed! Please can we lay down on the bed! I want to feel you laying on top of me!"

"Yeah, we can do that if you want. Yeah man! I'll lay on you and fuck the shit out of you if you want! Hell yes man! You have me so damn hot, you just tell me what you want to do!"

Bill grabbed ahold of Jim and told him, "I'm going to pull it out man. Stand still! I'm sure pulling it out will not feel like it did going in, but be ready. Ready?"

"Yeah man. Yeah, I'm ready, —pull it out! But please, please, —when we get to the bedroom, I want you to put it back in me right away again, OK?"

Bill rammed his dick in one more time, just as far as he could, then pulled it out and said. "Yeah, of course I'll fuck you again. You must like it, uh? You like having my stiff dick up in your butt, uh?"

"Oh yeah man! Yes, —I like it! I like it a lot! Yeah, —and when you pulled it out, it sure did not feel anything like when you pushed it up in me. When we get in the bedroom, I'm anxious to see how it feels going back in again. I bet it won't hurt like it did that first time! I kind of think my ass is used to it already!"

"Shit man, if you like it so much, I guess you had better plan on fucking my ass so I can see if I like it so much too! Will you?" Bill asked of his new bed-mate and sex-mate!

"Oh hell yes I will!' Jim anxiously replied. "Come on! Let's dry off and get in there! My ass is really wanting you up in there again! You've only been out of it for less than a minute, and I'm hungry for more already! Come on, lets do some more fucking and finding out what other stuff there is that we like to do. You know, —I think we have a lot of 'finding out' to do yet. I never thought I'd ever want to even think about some guy, —even just saying that he wanted to stick his cock up in my ass, but shit man, —I've got a completely different attitude about that now! What in the hell are we ever going to tell our wives, of what we did while they were gone? I hear some strong lies coming up!"

"You know what Bill?" Jim asked, as he displayed a little nervousness. "Now, I am really kind of wondering just what it might be like to put your dick in my mouth, too! Maybe let your thick dick kind of choke me a little bit! I, of course, know that gay guys do that to each other all of the time, but I never realized that us straight, married, guys might get all excited about doing it too!"

Jim continued, "Bill, —am I going too far in asking you if you want to stick your cock meat in my mouth? Bill, if I suck on your dick, or at least have it in my mouth, then I kind of think maybe I will have gone the whole way in doing some different and kind of exciting, stuff. Maybe that will let me know that I really went all the way, with getting some new, exciting actions tonight! Some exciting, —guy actions! Bill, I've always heard about this kind of stuff, but I've never done it. I never had anybody to do it with. I've always wondered about it though. I like to find new things to do, especially if they are kind of sexy things. Tonight I've got you! Bill, I'm liking what we are doing here tonight. They are really turning me on! Hey, if I can take your dick up in my ass, and let you fuck my asshole, as rough and a hard as you have, then, what's so much different about taking your dick down my throat? Have you ever thought about face fucking a guy before, Bill? Bill, will you face fuck me? —Please?"

CHAPTER THREE:

What a Trip, Man!

"Yes Jim, yes I will face fuck you!" Bill replied. "Jim I am so damned hot and anxious for some good playing together, I'm ready for anything that we can conjure up to try and do. Jim, I am so damn glad we found each other in the cafe tonight! Damn, I never had one iota of an idea that this week-end was going to turn out anything like this! Shit man, I am hot and I am ready and after what we have already done with each other, I don't think there is too much that we can't suggest to the other person. Jim, I have to admit it, —I have never, ever in my entire life, ever felt so completely open and available to tell some other person my real deep and naughty thoughts and desires like I am feeling with you tonight. I mean, Jim, I don't even tell my wife stuff like you and I are talking about tonight, let alone what we are doing together! I never do stuff like this with her. Oh Jim! What a great time! Come on man, let's get on that bed and let me get my dick up in your ass again!"

"I am going to finish fucking your ass, and then I am going to fuck your face, like you have been begging for, so man, —your ass and your mouth are both going to get it! So, get ready! Before tonight is over, you are really going to know what fucking is all about, —in both ends! Well, — maybe I should actually be saying, —before the night is over, 'WE' are going to know what fucking is all about, —in both ends! Giving and getting!"

Bill and Jim dried off, left the bathroom, and Bill pulled the bed covers down.

"Lay your ass down man, —lay your sweet ass down!" Bill instructed Jim.

Jim immediately hit the bed, stomach down and ass up.

"Hey Bill, put some more grease in my ass first, OK?"

"Yeah, I would if you needed any, but Jim my buddy, your ass is all greased up well enough, and I really don't think you need any more in there!"

And with that firm statement, Bill positioned himself above Jim's prone body, aimed his dick at Jim's asshole, and immediately entered in!

Man in man! Slam, bang, —-the two bodies came together! Bill hit the deck on Jim's ass! He didn't wait to see if Jim's ass was going to take it easy or not! He went in, —in one full push!

Jim obviously had no, nor expressed any, difficulty with taking Bill's dick with just the one slamming push! His ass was more than ready and anxious!

"Oh God Bill! Oh Bill! Oh shi—t man! Oh Bill, —fuck my ass, —Oh God Bill, fuck me! Fuck me crazy man!"

Bill grabbed Jim around the chest and laid his face down right beside Jim's neck. Bill turned slightly toward Jim, and gave his neck a slight kiss.

"Oh thanks man!" Jim said. "Oh Bill, —how in the hell can something as big as your dick feel so damn good to me, all up inside of my ass? Oh Bill! Why do I find this so damn great? Bill, —Oh Bill, —I love having you up in my ass! Oh fuck me pleaaa—se! Yeah, —fuck my ass man! Fuck me, fuck me!!"

Bill repositioned his legs to the outside of Jim's. He was straddling Jim's butt, he was fucking Jim's ass, he had his face turned toward Jim's neck, and almost in a whisper, very, very quietly, and very lovingly, saying,— "Jim, I'm fucking your ass man! Jim, I have my dick up in your butt man! I'm inside of you Sir! Jim, I'm fucking your asshole man! I'm having fun in your asshole man! Jim, you've never had some other guy up in your asshole before, have you Jim? Jim, baby, —I'm the first one to get to fuck your asshole, ain't I, Jim? Yeah, my dick up in there is the very first one, up in there, isn't it, Jim? You don't have a virgin ass anymore do you Jim? Your ass has now been fucked, hasn't it, Jim? Jim loves to have my dick up in there, doesn't he? Tell me you love having my dick up inside of you! Yeah, man, tell me!"

Jim turned toward Bill and suddenly gave him a kiss!

Bill's eyes opened in surprise, and he then quickly returned the kiss.

"Yeah Bill, my babe! Yeah, I have you up in my ass and Bill I am loving it! Bill your cock up in there is just great! Push it in me as far as you can please—-!"

"Hey Jim baby!" Bill said. "Hey, —is it OK if I call you 'Jim Baby' while I have my dick up inside of you? Jim, can I do that, man? Jim, right now I feel like we are a hell of a lot more than just neighborhood friends. Jim, tonight has really changed me, and I like the change. I really like the way I feel about you now. Jim, I'm glad you gave me that kiss! Jim, I feel like we are kind of one person now. Jim I've never felt this hot for anybody! Oh shit man! What have we started here tonight? Jim, I guess we have to admit that we are now fuck buddies, aren't we?"

"Bill, I don't know, but I do know it is all OK. Nothing that feels this good can be wrong, so for tonight, let's just enjoy our new found excitements and not let ourselves be all bothered about the what's, the ifs, and all that crap. Tonight, I just want to continue enjoying what we have found!"

Bill grabbed Jim and hugged him tightly! He gave Jim a number of unspoken kisses on the side of his neck, and continued to fuck his asshole. Fast, slow, gently, roughly! Bill used Jim's butt hole for all types of activity, and Jim encouraged them all.

As Bill continued his asshole playing, Jim could notice that Bill was becoming somewhat more self centered, not in a bad way, but rather in a good way, and Bill was picking up the speed and the rhythm of his fucking strokes. Bill was gabbing ahold of Jim even tighter than before, and Bill's breathing was starting to get very heavy and pronounced. Bill was humping and bumping fast and furious, he was breathing very strongly, and he was holding Jim very tightly! Jim was now getting a very serious fucking!

Jim could tell what was about to happen!

"Oh Jim, —oh Jim!" Bill exclaimed! "Oh Jim, I'm going to cum! Oh Jim, —oh Jim, I'm getting real ready to cum! Oh Jim, my dick is ragging hard! Jim, my dick is so hard it almost hurts!"

Bill was trying to tell Jim that he was almost to a climax, and at the same time continue to slam bang his ass and hold Jim to the point that Jim was about to loose any breathing capabilities, due to the tight squeeze.

"Oh Jim, —I'm cummmmin man! Oh man! Oh man! Oh Jim, —I'm cummmmin! I'm cumin! I'm cumin! Oh Jim, —oh Jim, I just came! Oh God, I just came! Oh Jim, I came! Oh shit man, I must have shot five or six times! Oh man, —Jim, I just shot you a whole ass full! Oh my God! My dick was so hard I wasn't sure it could shoot!"

Bill collapsed completely across Jim's body! He threw his hands up beside Jim's head. He laid his head down in exhaustion beside Jim's head. Be breathed deeply and heavily!

"Yeah I could tell," Jim kind of jokingly said. "Yeah, Bill my babe, I could feel it every time you shot me one. I think you shot more that just five or six times though. My, —I didn't know a man's cum is so warm. My ass is nice and warm now. Shit man, you really should be all drained now! You OK? Yeah Bill, my man, I think I agree. I should have an ass full right now, from what I felt hit the insides of me! How you feeling? You OK?"

"Oh yeah!" Bill managed to utter. "Yeah man! I'm OK. But shit man, I am fucking exhausted right now though! My body was so excited and ragging, and now it is all mush! Shooting off like that can totally wipe a guy out!"

"That's OK man!" Jim said. "Just lay there and rest. I like having you laying on me, so just lay there and we'll both kind of re-group here, OK?"

"Yeah, thanks man!" Bill replied.

Jim and Bill continued to lay there and enjoy the feel of the other man lying up against his own skin, for quite some time. They individually enjoyed the intimate and quiet time together. Bill started to re-coop and he took advantage of his being on top and having more mobility. He put a hand on each side of Jim's head and slightly rubbed it. He rubbed Jim's neck. As he moved his hands down the sides of Jim's torso, he continued his loving and caressing touching and slight rubbing. Bill then pulled his exhausted and limp dick out of Jim's ass, and he slid his body down the length of Jim's body. As he slid down, he licked the middle of Jim muscular back and enjoyed the deep indentation down the middle, created by the muscular back muscles that Jim so nicely displayed.

As Bill's face approached Jim's butt muscles, Bill moved his head to the left and took some butt muscle into his mouth.

He bit slightly. He heard Jim express a very pleasant moan. Bill moved to the right butt muscle and again took some muscle into his mouth. He again bit slightly. Jim again expressed a very, very happy moan. Bill then moved his mouth down so slightly on the same muscle and took another mouth full of butt. Once again, he bit so lovingly. Jim said, "Oh yeah, man! Oh yeah—! Yeah please do that again!"

Bill continued to follow his request for about six or eight more bites, and he then placed his face squarely in the crack of Jim's muscular butt muscles. He spread Jim's ass cheeks apart and he forced his face, down, in-between the butt cheeks! He shook his face back and forth! He pushed his face in farther. He again shook his face. He could feel Jim's butt cheeks moving side to side as he shook his face back and forth. He pulled his face out slightly to take a deep breath. He then re-entered the crevasse of Jim's butt. He stuck his tongue out. He licked the inside of Jim's left butt cheek. He heard Jim giving out some very enjoyable sounds of pleasure! This encouraged him to continue his actions to the right cheek. He heard more sounds of pleasure! He buried his face farther! He forced his face in between the butt cheeks. He extended his tongue out as far as he could and licked the tiny hole that he had just so recently pulled his dick out of. Jim let out some very exciting and some very acceptable moans and groans.

"Oh my God!" Jim almost yelled! "Oh my God Bill! Oh shit Bill! Oh, my God man! What a great feeling! Oh shit man! Oh my God, —I've never felt anything like that! Oh my God man, are you licking my asshole? Oh Bill, is that what I feel back there? Oh God man! Oh Bill, —oh shit man! What a great feeling!!!!! Oh Bill, lick me man, lick on me, —please!"

Bill continued to enjoy the confines of Jim's muscular butt structure, and before he re-surfaced for another deep breath of air, he licked the entire circle of Jim's ass hole, and most of the area surrounding it! For one very slight moment, he allowed his tongue to so very slightly enter the circular muscle of Jim's ass, and ever so slightly force it open and accept the tip of his tongue.

Having very secret realizations that he had just slightly licked the inside of Jim's ass hole, he wondered if Jim knew what had happened, and wondered if he should just keep quiet about it, or ask Jim if he knew that he had just stuck his tongue up in his ass. Bill did not know if putting your tongue up in a guy's ass was something to be proud of, and if so, should it be talked about? Bill was afraid that if doing that was something that nobody else would approve of, then why did he enjoy it so much? He did not know if he had kind of gone beyond the bounds of normal enjoyment.

He decided to kind of hint around the subject and see how Jim accepted it, if he could tell what had happened.

"You know Jim! For being a store manager, and having some job where a guy doesn't have to be a real hot body type of a guy, you sure as hell have managed to keep that body of yours looking like some high school jock! Man, I loved pushing my face right up in your ass like that! I had my face crammed in between two really strong and hot butt cheek muscles. Damn man! I never thought getting my face up in a guy's ass would be something to enjoy! Was I wrong! What a trip man!"

"Bill, that feeling you gave me when you did that was, —hot! What other word explains it! It was damn hot man! I've got to admit that I'm not sure I'd have the guts to put my tongue in a guy's ass hole, but hey, maybe when I have my face crammed up in your butt, maybe I'll know that is something that I need to do too. Bill, it felt great, damn great! Thanks for doing that!"

Bill felt relieved! He felt that his rather way out of bounds actions had been approved. And approved by the man that mattered! Bill knew that Jim was aware, and that Jim had not asked, "Why in the world, would any guy do that?"

"Hey Jim. I'm going into the bathroom and wash some of this grease off of my dick, and then I'm gonna fuck your mouth! So get yourself turned around on the bed there and when I get back, get ready for some hot 69 stuff! You asked me if I would, and I said yes, —so get all set man! I am about to face fuck you!

And, thinking about it, since I guess I will be having my mouth right about where your dick will be, then I guess maybe I will see what getting a big dick in my mouth is like too! You know, for two straight guys, we sure are having one hell of a good time with each other, aren't we?"

CHAPTER FOUR:

Two Straights Doing a '69'

Bill went to the bathroom and washed the grease off of his dick. As he dried it on a towel, he jerked it once or twice, and while shaking his head, realized to himself that he had just fucked the hell out of his buddy's ass! Smiling as he jerked it a couple of more times, he thought, "Oh shit man! Never, never, in the whole of time, did I ever think I would be fucking some guy's asshole, and on top of that, loving it as much as I did! Man! Oh shit man! Damn, I never dreamt that I would ever be doing this, and to Jim no less. Oh God man! Shit man! I loved it! It felt do damned good!"

As Bill continued to dry his cock meat off, or rather in a, — "lost world," kind of way, continued to jerk on it, he then realized, "Man! I'm going to go back in there and I am going to be putting his cock in my mouth, and he is going to be putting his in my mouth, and we are going to be sucking on each other's cocks! Shit man! I never thought I'd ever be doing that!"

As Bill processed his thoughts, he realized that he was getting very excited and very anxious to follow through with what he had just mentally processed,— as what was going to happen next. "Oh man! Oh man!" He thought to himself. "Oh shit man I never, ever thought I would be doing this! Oh shit man, why in the hell am I so damned anxious and so damned excited about it? Shit man! Men are not supposed to get this damned excited about putting another guy's dick in his mouth!"

Bill threw the towel on the back of the toilet tank, quickly turned, and headed for the bedroom.

"Oh Jim! Oh Jim! Man I feel like I am about to go crazy here man! Jim, just the thought of what we are going to be doing is getting my heart racing wild and crazy, man! Jim I never thought I would want to put a man's dick in my mouth, but my God man! I've got to suck on you, now!"

Jim was laying on his back, and his hard-on was looking like the Washington Monument! Straight up in the air!

Bill immediately threw himself down on the bed in the opposite direction from the way Jim was lying. Bill grabbed ahold of Jim's rod and immediately, without any hesitation at all, threw his mouth down on and around Jim's dick! He forced his mouth down on it as far as he could go!

Jim was shocked. He raised his head up far enough to look down toward his dick and Bill's mouth. "Shit man! Shit!" He exclaimed. "Shit man! God Bill! Man oh live! You sure were anxious for that, weren't you? Man! Bill I had no idea you were so ready to do that!"

Bill kind of pulled off of Jim's dick and took a deep breath. He then uttered the best that he could, since he still had the end of Jim's dick in his mouth, "Oh God man! Oh shit! Oh God, I just had to have this in my mouth! I had to have it! Jim, I got all crazy and just had to have it! Jim I had to get it! I had to have it in my mouth!"

"Well, you got it man!" Jim replied. "You have my dick in your mouth man! You've got it, man! How is it? I thought maybe we were going to kind of take each other at the same time, but I see there is no race now. How does that feel, Bill? You like having my dick in your mouth? How do I taste?"

Bill did not answer Jim's questions. He devoted his full attention to attempting to have Jim's cock in his mouth without gagging on it. He sucked on the end of it for a little while, and then he pushed his face down on it farther and farther to get more of it in his mouth. He would then suck on it again. Once or twice he forced the entire length of Jim's dick into his mouth. He quickly found out that to do that, and not be used to accepting all of it that far in, caused him some gagging and choking. He pulled back off far enough to be able to cough, but never letting the entire dick come completely out of his mouth.

Bill grabbed ahold of Jim's hips and pulled Jim closer to himself. He buried his face completely in Jim's crotch fuzz. All of a sudden, and during his first time of ever being on a man's dick, he trained himself on how to suck on a big cock, without so much as even taking the dick out of his mouth. Bill had unconsciously decided, apparently while rubbing his dick dry with the towel, that he was really ready to go get on Jim's cock and to learn how to master all techniques, —of how to make serious love to it. This had not been a conscious decision. As he was attempting to learn how to swallow the entire length of dick without gagging is when he rather mentally resurfaced and consciously realized what he was actually doing.

"Oh man! I'm on his dick! I'm sucking on Jim's dick! Shit man! I knew I was getting all really excited and anxious a few minutes ago, but shit man, I didn't know for sure that I was really going to actually suck on him! Man! What in the hell happened that I got on here so fast? Man, I must have kind of lost track of just what I was doing when I got myself all hot and bothered thinking about maybe doing this! Shit man! I thought I was just thinking about, —maybe, —maybe, doing this!"

Bill realized that he had actually lost his own self control over his internal excitement over just the shear thought of sucking on Jim's dick. Once he consciously realized that he was already doing it, then he decided that he needed to continue what he had already gotten started.

As Bill was ravaging Jim's dick, much to Jim's shocking surprise, Jim realized that Bill was in a world of his own, and any attempts to try and talk to him were completely needless! After the string of questions that Jim had asked, and gotten no reply from, Jim knew Bill was now in, "another place".

Although not being quite as overtaken with such an unconscious anxiety, Jim was very eager to start his own adventures onto Bill's meat rod. "Shit man!" He thought to himself. "I'm the one that was kind of begging to get face fucked, and he is the one that didn't even wait for me to kind of even ask him if I could put my dick in his mouth! Man he grabbed mine and he took mine like an old pro! He went down on mine like he knew all of the what's and all of the how's."

Jim attempted to divide his attention between the great feeling, and the unexpected excitement, of having Bill so eagerly eating his dick, and at the same time experience his own personal excitement of knowing that he was about to put some guy's dick in his own mouth, and,—for his very first time ever! He had ahold of Bill's dick, and he so ever slowly moved his mouth toward it. As he continued to enjoy the excitement of what was actually happening to his own dick, he extend his tongue out and very gently started to lick on the side of Bill's rod. As he did, he realized, "Oh shit man! I'm acting like I'm afraid to lick the side of his dick, and he slammed his mouth down on my dick without so much as even acting like it was something different and new for him. Man, I'm a wimp! I'm the one that was begging from him to face fuck me!"

Suddenly Jim was hoping that Bill was totally unaware that he had not yet taken Bill's dick into his mouth. He did not want Bill to know that he had not pounced onto Bill's stick, as suddenly and as quickly as Bill had done to his. Jim took a deep breath, realized that this was something very strange and different to himself, but also decided that he needed to "get with the show," if he did not wish to have to attempt any kind of an explanation to Bill, that he had found it kind of intimidating and kind of scary to put his mouth on another guy's dick.

Jim opened his mouth wide, aimed Bill's meat rod directly toward his mouth and after closing his eyes, he forced a quick movement of his head. His mouth fell directly onto Bill's dick! Suddenly he had a mouth full of dick! He attempted a deep breath through his mouth and quickly realized that breathing through his mouth, with it full of cock, was not a workable thing to do. He pulled his mouth off of Bill's dick. He moved his head back some, took a deep breath, which was necessary only due to his heavy nervous breathing, and looked at the dick that he had just had in his mouth! He took a second deep breath, and once again put his mouth down on the stiff, thick, meat rod. He took a deep breath through his nose. He pushed his mouth down farther. He heard Bill almost yell, "Yeah! Yeah!"

Jim did not know for sure if that was a reaction to the new feeling of having his mouth completely surrounding Bill's dick, or if it was a reaction to something that Bill was doing, at that very same time, to Jim's rod! Jim knew that either reaction was good! He knew that Bill was giving him some great feelings too! Some feelings that would make him yell, "Yeah, Yeah," if he had not been so consumed in mentally accepting the fact that he was actually putting another guy's dick in his mouth, and, —he was attempting to put as much of it in there as possible.

Bill was going after Jim's dick like this could have been the third or fourth one this day! He was demonstrating a complete accomplishment in cock sucking.

Jim was much more reserved in attending to Bill's rod, and he was taking the process much slower. He slowly moved his head back and forth in small motions, and treated Bill's meat stick as if it might break, —if too fast of an action was placed on it. Slowly he gained more and more comfort in knowing that his actions on it were not putting it in any danger. His actions got more and more active, and less and less guarded.

Bill pulled off of Jim's stick of cock meat and said, "Yeah man! That feels good! Yeah, Jim, suck on me hard! Yeah man! Make me know you've got me in your mouth! Suck me man, suck me!"

As Bill resumed his proper position taking care of Jim's cock, both men gained additional motions and additional force in taking care of the other man's stick of meat. Jim had gained considerable confidence that he was doing what was right, and he had finally lost his uncomfortable feeling about having some other guy's cock stuck down his throat.

Jim pulled off and asked. "Hey Bill. Am I doing OK down here? Can you feel me on your dick? Is this OK?"

"Oh, hell yes it is quite OK!" Bill replied. "It feels damn good man. My dick is so damn hard again it almost hurts again. Jim, suck and chew on me! Kind of bite my dick so I can really feel you doing me! Yeah, yeah! That feels so damn good to me, it is really getting me all hot, man!"

Jim and Bill were is the typical '69' position. Jim's head was down toward the foot of the bed and Bill's head was up toward the head of the bed. Both men had good strong holds on his bed partner. Both suckers had successfully managed to take the full length of his partner's dick. Bill of course, with his initial action of attacking Jim's meat without even consciously realizing what he was actually doing, was the quicker man to suck the visiting cock down into his throat as fast as it could possibly go, but once Jim got past his being squeamish about having some guy's dick in his mouth, he made up some lost time, and was quickly demonstrating comparable capabilities to Bill's sucking actions.

The two men were totally attached to each other, and at one time almost rolled off of the side of the bed during one of their more active actions of loving, —the feel of the man, —the feel of the cock in the mouth and, —the reality of actually having part, and especially that particular part, of his close friend in his mouth!

The mouths of both men were getting a very serious workout! Both men were excited and were acting in a very dramatic manner! Both men were completely, and very actively into this face fucking!

Suddenly Bill pulled off of Jim's meat and said, "Oh, hey man! Just in case you have not noticed yet, you are getting a good strong face fucking! I am fucking your face, man! You wanted a good face fucking, —right? You wanted my cock in your mouth, —right? You wanted me to fuck your face, —right? Well man, —let me fuck your face some more then!"

And with that statement, Bill resumed fucking Jim's mouth with an even more aggressive mouth fucking.

Jim pulled off for only a quick second and said, "You are getting a fast face fucking too, and from the way I am feeling right now, you are just about to see what my cum tastes like because man, —I am just about ready to let it all fly man! Bill, I am getting really close to cumin man, —ya man, —ya man, —Bill, —Bill, —it's cumin man, —it's cummmmin!"

With excited exclamation, Jim clamped down tightly on Bill's dick, grabbed ahold of Bill's head and as he pulled Bill's head up tightly to his body, he exploded into Bill's mouth. He pushed his dick into Bill's face as far as he could. Bill attempted to get as much air as he could by breathing through his nose. He felt the warm and forceful cum hit the back of his throat. He immediately started swallowing it as quickly as he could since he knew that he would not be able to pull his mouth off of Jim's dick if his mouth got too full!

Exactly at the same time, Bill had an identical physical reaction, and his load started exploding into Jim's mouth. Jim gagged but had no other option than to suffer through the explosion in his mouth, and to swallow it as quickly as possible, and to then attempt to get some air into his lungs.

Both men remained strongly attached to the other man! Both by having the other man's dick in his mouth, but also by having a complete, firm, and a total body hold on the other man, as each man gasped for as much air as he could get.

Cum was dripping from the mouth of each man, and both men were hugging the other man, as tightly as he could, as if he expected the other one to attempt, to get up and get away. Neither man had any desire to separate from the other. Neither man had any desire or wish to get out of bed! Both men hugged and kissed any and all body parts that they could easily reach.

"Oh Jim! Oh Jim!" Bill finally uttered. "Oh Jim, this is just too great! Jim I never, and I do mean never, thought that I would ever have a man's dick stuck down my throat, and I sure as hell never thought that I'd ever have a mouth full of cum from some other guy either, but Jim, this has been great! I don't know if it could have been this great if it had been with another guy or not, but Jim, please promise me that we can do this as often as possible. Jim I have never experienced anything as exciting as this has been. God man! For just thinking that we were just going to jack off together, —this night sure has changed me! Oh Jim, I don't want us to let loose of each other!"

"You know Jim. I'm not just sure how we are going to be able to work this out, but I know damn well that if you are as anxious to do this again and maybe as often as I am, we have to do something that makes it work. Jim, this night has been way beyond belief for me. I never thought I could feel this way, and to think that it all happened just because we both happened to be at Jack's Cafe & Bar at the same time tonight. Hey, I still want to give you a good asshole fucking! You still up to that? I thought we were going to do that earlier, and we got ourselves all tied up in this sucking each other thing, but if you are still game, I really do want you to find out how great getting a dick up in the ass feels. You still up for it?"

"Shit yes man! I am! Hell I'm afraid to pass up anything tonight! I've never expected anything like this to happen, and now that it has man, —I want everything! Yeah man! Yeah, I wanna know that I had you up in my ass man! Jim, this whole thing is turning out way too exciting to even believe it is real! Jim, I always thought I was just a straight guy, but man, I really wonder now!"

"Let me get up and run through the shower for just a second. If you want to shower some too, I'm going to put on some fresh sheets while you are showering. We've got cum all over these. Just imagine! Us two straight guys getting cum all over the sheets together! I think we may need to reconsider just exactly who we really are after this night! And if it's at all possible, I really do want you to stay here with me tonight! Can you do that? If I change the bed sheets before you fuck my ass, then if you'll stay here tonight, we can just cuddle up together and kind of feel each other up as we go to sleep. Can you stay here? There's no reason you have to be at the house is there?"

"No, I don't have to be there. Yeah, hell yes I will stay! Thank God you offered because if you hadn't, then I was going to have to get real gutsy and just ask if I could. I told Janice before she left that I might, just might, go up to the cabin for part of the week-end and do some fishing, so if anybody happens to call the house, —that is where I am! No phone at the cabin, so nobody can call there anyway! Shit yes man, I am staying here with you! Fuck your cute little ass Bill, and let you know what it really feels like to be a real man, with a big dick stuck up in there, and then love on you all night long! Hey, go hit the shower. I'll pull these sheets off while you do that. Don't take too long, cause I'm real anxious to fuck that cute butt of yours! I'm going to take your ass cherry man! I am going to fuck my, — 'straight,' buddy!"

CHAPTER FIVE:

Yeah, Push on it Man!

As Bill came back into the bedroom from taking his quick shower, he brought in some additional bed sheets and with Jim's help, re-made the bed.

"Hey, don't let me forget to throw these dirty sheets in the washer and wash them up and get them back on this bed, or I am really going to have some damn serious explaining to do when Sue gets home and finds some ole cum spots all over them. I think I'll let them lay here on the floor, kind of in the way, so that I remember them tomorrow morning." Bill told Jim, —as they finished re-making the bed.

"Yeah man! Let 'em lay right there and you lay yourself down right here!" Jim replied. "It is now time for me to do some serious ass fucking, and it is fucking your sweet little ass! I am really looking forward to this. I'm hard and ready! Shit man! Just a few hours ago there is no way in hell that I would have even dreamt of laying on the top of some guy and ramming my dick up in his ass, but God how things can change in just a matter of moments. Not only am I going to ram a guy's ass, it's going to be my buddy Bill's ass! Shit man! I can't believe this! Wow—the way things change! Yeah, and to think that all we were supposed to be doing with each other here tonight was feeling each other as we jerked ourselves off! Man! Did that concept ever go out the freaking window fast! But hey, I'm sure not complaining any! Are you?"

"Hey Jim." Bill said. "Yeah, I'm ready, but I've got to ask you to really go easy on me. I know you found out that you really liked having my cock up in your ass man, —but man, —you've got to remember that I've never been butt fucked before, and I've got to admit that right now I'm still a little worried about just what in the hell it is going to feel like having something rammed up into my ass. Jim, you've got to remember that until tonight I had never even stuck my own finger up in my ass before! When you finger fucked me earlier in the shower, that is the first time that anything ever went up in my ass. Hell, —you know what? Unless I was just a baby, I don't even remember of even getting a rectal thermometer put up in my ass. I've only used that thing for shitting out of."

"Bill my boy. You just lay there and relax. You are going to be quite OK. You've got to trust me. OK? You just stretch out there and relax. Everything back here is going to be all right. In just a few minutes you will be begging me to fuck you faster and deeper, so right now, just trust me, OK? Your ass is going to be OK."

"Yeah, OK!" Bill answered. "Jim, I trust you, I'm just nervous about getting that rod of yours up in my butt. Jim, you have to admit that you've got a whole lot bigger dick than I do, so you're going to be putting more, —a hell of a lot more meat up in me, than I did with you!"

"Yeah, yeah, I know! Listening to you, a person would think I was hung like a fucking horse! It's just a little man dick, and soon you are going to be wishing it was a hell of a lot bigger than it is! Lay still man. Stretch your arms out, up by your head.

I'm going to grease your ass up and then I will go in it real slow, and real nice. OK? You OK?"

"Yeah, Jim. I'm OK, I'm just nervous though. Got to admit! No way in hell would I have ever thought, earlier today, that I'd be getting ass fucked before the night was over. Jim, I just don't understand it. Knowing that I was going to be ramming my dick up your asshole sure didn't make me nervous, it just made me excited, but knowing that I'm the one getting my asshole rammed now, is kind of a different thing. Oh, hey! When I greased up your ass I kind of found out that I should have had a rag or some paper towels close by, to wipe my greasy hand on, so I brought in that small green towel over there for you to use, if you want."

"OK Bill. I saw that and kind of figured that is why you brought it in. Now lay there and relax your butt. Just by touching it, I can tell you have got it all slammed shut. Just relax it and let me do my thing back here. OK? Bill, if you really don't want to follow through with this once I get started, you let me know and we can stop. That's what I had asked of you before you fucked me, so I kind of guess I should agree to the same thing. But, you are going to be OK man!"

Jim greased up Bill's ass and before wiping his hand off with the towel, put some grease on his own dick and jerked it back and forth a few times in anticipation of getting it up in a guy's ass for the very first time. He was anxious to start fucking a man's butt, and the man was his buddy Bill. As anxious as he was, he wondered to himself if he had really been wanting to do this for a long time now, —but just never consciously realized it.

With Bill laying prone on his stomach and with his hands reaching up above his head, Jim laid down on Bill's back and by reaching down, he slid his hard-on dick down between Bill's legs and right up to the bottom of his ass cheeks. He reached up and placed his hands on top of Bill's hands, and then slowly pulled his hands back down, feeling Bill's arms, his shoulders and his back as he slid his hands back toward himself.

Slowly Jim rubbed Bill's back, shoulders, and the under side of his upper arms. He slowly lowered his face and gently kissed the back of Bill's neck, he kissed the upper parts of each arm, and then slowly slid his tongue down the length of Bill's muscular back. As he was licking Bill's back, he continued to massage Bill's shoulders and the bottom of his neck.

He continued his tongue action down the middle of Bill's back and licked the width of Bill's narrow waist line, and then continued on down to the top of Bill's butt muscles. He licked and then he slightly chewed on Bill's firm butt. He made love to each side of Bill's ass. He licked, he kissed, and he chewed on each side. He slightly slid the tip of his tongue in between Bill's butt cheeks and then slowly drew it up the middle of Bill's back.

Jim worked his way back up the length of Bill's torso. He licked and kissed his way back to Bill's broad shoulders and kissed as deeply as he could, each arm pit. He bit some of Bill's arm pit hair in his teeth, and slightly pulled on it as he moved his head. As he withdrew from each arm pit, he so very gently and lovingly bit and sucked on Bill's upper back and shoulders, right at the spot where his arms meet his back.

Jim heard Bill express some very deep pleasures with some very meaningful moans and groans. Jim knew that each moan and groan was a sound and an expression of pleasure and acceptance. He also knew that each sound was actually a pleading for more of the same. Jim knew that Bill's ass was connected to the upper part of his body, and the pleasure that he was experiencing up higher on his body, was getting the lower part of his body all ready and excited to receive its first cock fucking. Jim could feel Bill's lower torso raise and lower as if begging for some lower body action. He didn't know if Bill was actually aware that his butt was starting to react to the actions or not, but he did know that regardless of if Bill knew it or not, that it was definitely a signal, that ass action was now being begged for. It was being begged for, and he was ready and anxious to deliver. He remembered how greatly sweet it had been for him only such a short time earlier when Bill had his cock rammed up in his butt, and he was now anxious to let Bill feel the same new and exciting feelings. The feelings of a man's big and stiff cock rammed up into his ass as far as possible! The feelings of one man, being inside of another man. The feelings of man to man, —muscle to muscle, —strength to strength!

Slowly Jim raised his own mid-body section up so slightly, grabbed his blood filled stiff rod, aimed it for Bill's hole, and so very slowly and gently started to lower himself down, onto, and into, Bill.

Jim actually mentally realized to himself that, "I am actually going to be putting my cock up in Bill's ass. He is a friend of mine. A guy that I have known for a few years, and I am now going to ram his asshole with my dick! Somebody that I have known in the community and in city meetings, or perhaps have talked to in a neighborhood store. He is somebody that I have never, ever, even wondered what he looks like without clothes on. Somebody that I have never had any sexual questions about. Somebody that I should have never been sexually interested in. Shit man, —this is sure something that I never thought could or would ever happen! I never even thought about playing with another guy and his cock, or his ass, or having another guy play with mine, and especially some guy I already knew! Hell, I don't think I would have even liked the idea, if some guy had come up to me and told me he wanted to do that! I'd probably have gotten mad at him. I'm actually going to fuck Bill's ass! I'm actually going to stick my cock up in his ass! I'm a man! He's a man! We are both straight guys! Or at least we are supposed to be! I can't believe it! I can not believe that he and I are actually fucking each other like married people do to each other! Never in my entire life did I ever play with the idea of pushing my dick up in some guy's ass, and here I am, using Bill's ass! He has fucked me, and he really fucked me good! He has had his cock up in my ass and I loved it! He has shot his wad up in me, and I'm sure I will be doing the same thing to him when I fuck his ass. I've sucked on his cock and he has sucked on mine! I've cum in his mouth and he has cum in mine! I've grabbed his head and held on tight, and pulled him up close to my body when I shot in his mouth. I made him take my cum, —but he wanted it! He was anxious, too! I'm now laying on him and his bare ass. I'm laying on a completely naked man, and I'm about to stick my cock up in him! I'm hugging and kissing him. I'm biting on him and I'm biting his ass. I'm actually biting another guy's ass! My God, before this, I wouldn't even have touched another guy's ass! I'm kissing his arm pits. I'm putting my face right in his arm pits. I'm licking his butt and his butt crack! I'm making true love to him! I'm truly making real love to this man! I'm using him and his butch body, and he is using me, and my body, and we are both loving it! This is way too much to realize is true and actually happening! I love to feel him. I love his strong body up against mine. I've never wanted to hug another guy before, but oh man, I love to have him in my arms! I feel like I'm in a dream! I can not believe this, I can't! I never expected anything like this to happen! Never!"

Jim was just about to do his first ever guy fucking, and Bill was just about to get a cock up and in his ass, for his very first time. As had been going on all night, ever since they happened to find each other at the cafe, they were continuing to experience more and more, 'first time' activities. Every activity that they undertook was a completely new experience, since neither man had ever played sexually with another guy before. And both men knew that he, personally, had never had the desire to play with another guy before. Something new was happening to both men at this time, and they were both happy for it. Happy ass hell man, happy as hell! They were each excited about their new sexual connection to each other. Totally unexpected, but who cared now?

"Relax your butt, Baby." Jim so very softly said to Bill. "I want to make love to your ass Baby! I want to get into your ass and make love to you, —and to it, too! I'm going to let you know what it is like to have a man make love to you! You did that for me earlier tonight, and now it is my turn to return the favor!"

Jim could actually tell, that Bill had heard the request, and had attempted to make his butt muscles relax as much as possible. He knew Bill was still nervous about having a big dick shoved up into his ass. He knew that he needed to go slow, real slow and careful, so that Bill didn't freak out and beg out of getting fucked.

"You're OK man. I've got the head of my dick right at your asshole and I'm going to start sliding it in you real nice and slow. I'm going to be real careful with your ass. This is not going to hurt any, and it is going to feel real good going in. You relax your ass and you will be glad that you are getting my dick up in you. I promise not to hurt you any. I put a lot of grease up in your ass, and I've got some on my dick. It will feel different, but I promise to not hurt you any. Once you take it, you will be really glad!"

Bill took a deep breath and attempted to relax his entire body on the bed. Jim slowly and gently started the entrance into Bill's ass. He slowly pushed the head of his dick in Bill's asshole. He had gone into Bill's ass. The head of his dick had penetrated. Bill let out an excited moan. Not a moan of pain, but rather a pure moan of nervous excitement. Jim could feel Bill's heart beating. It was beating hard!

Jim put his arms around Bill's chest and hugged him firmly. "I'm in you man! I'm in your ass! My dick is in you! See, —you're OK!"

Again slowly, Jim pushed his body toward the young muscular body that was stretched out on the bed beneath him. His nine inch dick protruded into Bill's ass another inch or two. Bill kind of threw his head up and he moaned. Once again he moaned with a nervous pleasure.

"Oh Jim. Yeah Jim! That is feeling good. How much of your dick have you got in me? How far in are you?"

"Hey man! I'm just getting started back here. I've only got a little of it in you so far. You just lay there and relax yourself, and give me some time, and I'll get some more up in there. You are feeling OK, —right?"

"Oh yeah, I'm feeling fine! I'm feeling fine! Jim, I was getting kind of afraid of actually getting fucked by you and that damn big dick of yours, but yeah, —it is feeling really good now. Tell me when you have it all the way up in me, OK?"

"Yeah, I will Bill, —but I've got a long way to go yet. You've only got the end of it in there right now, so just lay there and let me do you. Let me have your ass. Let me play with it and I'll let you know when you've got the whole thing."

As Jim laid on top of Bill's body, he continued to slowly push more and more of his hard rod up, and into Bill's ass. He hugged Bill around the chest, he kissed Bill's shoulders and upper arms. He kissed Bill's neck and then laid his head down beside Bill's face and gently kissed Bill on the chin as he prepared to push the rest of his dick up into Bill's ass.

The last push was quite more forceful and considerably more quickly done, than any of the earlier movements had been. He allowed the last five inches, or so, of his dick to enter and find its home in Bill's ass, with somewhat of a slight rush. He grabbed Bill strongly as he actually rammed the rest of his cock up and into Bill's ass. He knew Bill was ready for it, and wanted it. Bill had been kind of moaning, "Yeah man! Yeah man!" Jim knew from that, that Bill's ass was hungry for the rest of his cock, and was wanting it, all of a sudden.

"Oh God! Oh God!" Bill just almost yelled out loud. "Oh God Jim, you have all of it up in me now don't you? Oh God Jim! Oh Jim, —yeah, —push on it man! Oh Jim! Oh God man! Oh shit that feels so damn good up in me. Oh God man! My ass feels so full! Oh shit man! Fuck me! Yeah, Jim, —please, please fuck me now! Oh fuck me! Oh Jim I'm not afraid anymore. Oh man! I'm getting fucked! Oh shit man! I'm getting fucked! Jim, now that I know I can take that whole damn thing, fuck me like some raging idiot! Oh shit man! Oh shit man!! Oh Jim, —I knew I really did want you up in there, I was just nervous and kind of afraid that it was going to hurt, having that much dick pushed up in me, but oh man, it feels so good now! Oh Jim, —push on my body! Push on me! Let me feel you pushing on me as hard as you can!"

Jim grabbed Bill around the chest and hugged him as tightly as he could. He pushed his mid-section up against Bill's ass as firmly as he could. He kissed Bill right beside his left eye and said, "Yeah man! Yeah, you now have it all. I'm pushing it up in there as far as I can, and right now I wish it was about 10 inches longer. It feels so damn good up in there that I wish I had more to give you."

"Oh shit man! Oh God Jim! I'm not sure I could take any more than what is up in there right now, but Jim that does feel so good! Oh Jim. I've never felt anything like that before! Yeah, —oh you sure are right! Yeah, once you get it up in there, it sure does feel good! Oh man! Shit man! Jim, I can tell already that this is not going to be the only time I get fucked! I guess I'm into some new stuff in my life, but I know one thing man,—no woman will ever be able to do this for me! Jim, don't ever move out of town man. I'm going to be needing your dick a lot, and I'm going to be needing it often, I'm sure. Oh Jim, fuck me! Let me feel you pump my butt! Let me feel what it is really like to get a real strong guy fucking back there! Oh Jim I am so glad you are up in me! Oh man! Yeah—fuck the hell out of me now! Oh God Jim! There is no way in hell, that when I went into that cafe this evening did I ever imagine that before the night was over I would be almost yelling at some guy to fuck me! God Jim! Fuck me! —Fuck me! —Fuck me! Oh shit man! Just saying that, feels almost too weird and too funny to actually be begging that. I'm actually begging for you to fuck my ass! I'm begging a guy to give me a fucking in the ass! Never have I ever thought that I'd ever have sex with some other guy, let alone, begging him to fuck my ass, and to fuck it hard! Oh Jim! What a day this has turned out to be! Oh Jim, I love this! Fuck me man! Fuck my ass!"

Jim did not reply to Bill, but did respond with the begged for actions. He raised himself up slightly from on Bill's back, braced himself, and did as he was begged to do. He fucked Bill, and he fucked Bill quickly and forcefully. He made the bed shake with the fast and furious action that he was treating Bill's ass to. He heard Bill almost yelling for, "More, more!" — and he attempted to follow the request.

Bill had taken to getting his ass fucked, very, very quickly. As Jim was pounding him, he realized that getting fucked in the ass was some kind of a natural for him. He remembered what Jim had said about wishing he had another 10 inches to ram up in there, and Bill was actually thinking the same thing right then. "Oh shit man! Yeah, —I wish he had another 10 inches too. What he has got up in me right now is so damn good, I wonder what another 10 inches could feel like. Shit, I wish I could know!"

Jim was quickly finding out that fucking some guy's ass was just as much fun as getting fucked. He had a new pleasure in life, and he was using every opportunity offered to him, to make the most out of it. He was seriously finding out that being a fucker or being a fuckee, were both great positions to be in. Fantastic positions! Either one, —and both!

The two new sex partners, as they had now accepted to be thought of, —at least between the two of them, continued to fuck with all of the joy and excitement, that two guys, —two guys that had never even pondered what having sex with another guy would be like, could manifest. They were enjoying the new found feelings of having another man in bed with himself, and enjoying the newly discovered pleasures of feeling, in the most intimate of ways, the strong body structure of another man. Having that man in his bed, —having that man in his hands, —having that man in his mouth and having that man in his ass!

Bill reached over toward the bed stand and turned off the lamp. "Don't get off of me! Stay there! Stay in me! Fuck me! Fuck me until you cum! Load my ass up with your cum, and then stay in there and let me go to sleep with you up in my ass. I want to sleep with you still in me, if possible. I want to wake up tomorrow morning with your cock still up in my ass."

"Hey Mr. Bill! I sure will stay in you until I cum, and if I'm as successful at stopping my cum shots as I think I am, I'll be in there for a long time yet tonight. As far as you waking up with my dick up in your ass tomorrow morning, all I need to do is make sure I wake up before you do, because if I do, I'm sure you will be waking up while you are getting a good morning fucking!"

With Jim still on top of Bill, and still in Bill's ass, he gave Bill a big bear hug, and told him to lay still while he fucked him to sleep.

As Bill turned his face, as far as possible, to attempt a kiss on Jim's face, he said, "Fuck me man! Yeah, fuck me to sleep, and then fuck me awake again in the morning. Jim, I am going to thank God forever that you had the guts to ask me if I knew where you could go to get some sex, and I am so glad I had the guts to suggest we just kind of play with each other while we jerked off. Never had I ever before, played with the idea of having some guy fucking my ass, or me fucking his, but damn I am so glad it has happened. And I am so glad it is you, that it happened with. Good night man. Fuck me!"

A Boner Book

CHAPTER SIX:

Early Morning, The Day After

The two men woke up early the next morning. As each man looked at his bed mate, Jim and Bill both broke out into wide grins. The grins were for a multitude of reasons.

Jim and Bill had experienced some of their most exciting times of their lives with each other the night before, and each man had discovered exactly how fantastic it was to have the opportunity to explore and experience the complete and full relationship, friendship wise and sexually, with another man.

As they so slightly woke up and grinned at each other, Bill remarked to Jim. "Oh shit man! Of God man, you really are here! Jim, I guess the fact that you are in bed with me here, does mean that what I thought I had dreamed, was a reality. We really did do that stuff, right?"

Jim reached out, put his hand around Bill's chest, moved over toward him closer and replied, "Well, —I sure as the hell guess we did! Bill, I've got to admit that until you said something to me, I was still laying there trying to clear my head enough to understand if I was coming out of a real deep dream, or if I was really where I thought I was. Bill, I thought it was a dream too. Damn man, I am sure glad it wasn't! Shit man, if that had been a dream, I would have tried my damnedest to go back to sleep to restart it all over again. Bill, I am having trouble actually realizing that, what I remember, is what we did. Never in my entire life did I ever dream of doing that, nor as far as I can remember, even think that I wanted to. Bill, —what a night! How is your ass feeling? You OK?"

"Yeah, it's OK. But now that I can kind of start remembering stuff, I think I wanted to wake up with you, up in my ass this morning, didn't I? I kind of remember that just before we went to sleep last night, I told you that I wanted to wake up this morning by getting fucked in the ass again. Jim, we went to sleep with your dick up in my ass, didn't we?"

"Yeah, Bill. Yeah, I guess we did. I remember that I had my dick up in you when you tried to turn far enough to give me a kiss, and I remember that I was on top of your back, and yeah, I had my dick up in you, but I don't remember ever pulling it out. Yeah, —I guess we must have. I wonder how long I laid there with it up in your ass! I guess I fell asleep that way. Shit man, I wish I knew how long I laid on top of you like that."

"It would be kind of interesting to know, wouldn't it?" Bill replied. "Oh, say, there is still some grease in that bowl over there if that happens to be of any interest to you, in following through with your part of my request, of last night. I can always act like I am asleep and then you can wake me up by fucking me awake!"

"Bill, let me go take a piss and then I'll take advantage of that grease, but I've got to take my normal early morning piss first! Whenever I get up, the very first thing I always have to do, is go take a good piss. Lay still hot ass, —I will be right back!"

Jim got up, went to the bathroom and took his piss. Bill stretched himself out full length of the bed, with his ass showing

58

and glowing completely, and his arms and hands stretched up above his head.

As Jim re-entered the bedroom, Bill told him. "I was kind of wishing I had a pencil and a piece of paper really handy while you were in the bathroom. I wanted to put a note on my back that said, "Enter Here" with an arrow pointing at my ass!"

"No note necessary!" Jim answered. "Everything I did last night was something completely new to me, —and exciting to me, —but I do remember where I found your cute little asshole."

And as Jim laid down on Bill's back, he grabbed some grease, smeared it on his dick and told Bill, "Last night I went nice and slow going in there, just so you would know you can take it, but buddy, today is a new day! We know damn well how anxious you got for this hot dog up in your butt last night, so today I am going in, and I am going in all at once! You ready?"

"Yeah, I'm ready, well, —I think I'm ready!"

"You better be Mr. Bill, because I sure as the hell am, and I am coming in. Hang on man, —I'm gonna fuck you, and fuck you good!"

Bill immediately placed the tip of his rod right at Bill's asshole and pushed. He pushed fully and completely. He rammed Bill's ass. Bill jumped and almost yelled out. He did loudly moan a very pronounced moan of, "Ohhhhhhhhh!" He threw his hands up higher on the bed. He jerked his torso. He twisted and jerked for a moment.

"Oh shit man! Oh shit! Oh God, my ass must have tightened up again. Oh shit!! Jim, just lay on me there for a minute! Oh shit Jim! God your dick feels bigger today than it did last night!"

Jim laid down on Bill and asked. "You OK man? You OK? I'm sorry! I really didn't think it was going to hurt you that much this morning. Bill, I'm sorry. I just plain got too damn horny for your butt! Bill I'm sorry!"

"Hey, man, my fucker man! Don't worry about it. It's gone, and Jim I have to tell you that since I know how damn good your dick feels up in me, I have to admit that if I knew that is what I had to expect every time, I'd just accept it just to get your dick up in me. Jim, I have to admit that for being some straight guy, I do have to admit to you that I have now found out that I love having that damn big thing up in me. Jim, I'm starting to worry about me. Right now I'm feeling like it's more fun, and more exciting, and —I like getting it in the ass, better than I like doing the woman fucking. Jim, men are not supposed to feel that way, are we?"

"Bill, I really don't know. You and I sure have discovered some really exciting stuff since yesterday afternoon, and maybe it's just because it's new stuff to us, but yeah I know what you are saying. This is way too exciting for me too! I'm like you. We, being the straight guys that we are, we're not supposed to like this so damn much are we? Hey, Bill, all I can say is, let's enjoy ourselves while we have the chance, and then we can decide later, after all of our huffing and puffing each other has cooled off for awhile, what we feel then. Hey man, we might, both, just realize that this was kind of like teen-age exploring, which I sure know I never had the chance to do. Maybe we just happened to be a couple of guys that are getting around to this kind of playing around a little later in life than most guys. Tell you what, —for right now, —you just lay there and let me use your asshole and let me fuck the hell out of you! If it turns out later that we both agree this was a week-end never to be talked about again, then while we are doing it, let me enjoy it to the utmost, because right now, all I can say is, I'm horny for your manly-ass, and I want to fuck the hell out of it! OK?"

"Yeah, OK." Bill answered. "You're right Jim. In a couple of days, we might be kind of hesitant to even see each other, we might both feel guilty of what we did this week-end, but for right now, let's play like kids and you fuck the hell out of me!"

With that statement, Jim and Bill resumed the fucking that they were both so anxious to do. Bill offered his ass and attempted to make this fucking as good and exciting to his top man as he could. Jim slammed, rammed and banged Bill's ass as forcefully as he could. He grabbed Bill around the chest and hugged him as he slammed his ass. He pumped Bill's ass trying to get Bill to beg for some slowdown, but it never happened. The faster and the harder Jim fucked, the more Bill would groan and moan for "More! Fuck me harder!"

All of a sudden, they heard a board crack. It sounded like a broken baseball bat.

"Oh shit!" Bill said. "Oh shit! I think we just broke one of the bed slats! Shit man! Didn't that sound to you like one of the bed slats cracking?"

"Yeah Bill, it did! Have you got wooden slats under the springs on this bed?"

"Yeah, yeah we do. I think our actions finally got the best of one of those boards. Maybe we had better either take it a little more calmly or put me on the floor. I guess I just got fucked hard enough to break the bed!"

"Yeah, you did man, and so that we don't have to rebuild a bed before the day is over, I like the idea of getting you down on the floor. I haven't downloaded into your ass yet, and I'm not going to stop fucking you till I've drained all of my morning cum, —so let's finish this on the floor!"

Jim got off of Bill's backside and the two moved to the floor, and immediately got back in action.

"Shit man!" Bill exclaimed. "Shit! Everything we are doing is so damn exciting! Who in the hell would have thought that just the idea of fucking me on the floor, instead of on the bed, would make me feel so excited again, —like we are doing something that is really on the weird, bad, and exciting side. Shit man! On the bed or on the floor! What's the difference? But to me, —now this kind of makes me feel like we are fucking outdoors or something. Jim, this is exciting! I feel like we are doing stuff where we are not supposed to be doing it!"

"Bill, —Bill!" Jim quickly answered back. "Bill, —you just said it! You just said it!"

"I said what? What in the hell are you saying Jim?"

"Bill, —fucking outdoors! Bill you want to get fucked outdoors? Bill, I want to fuck you outdoors!"

"Jim what in the hell are you saying? There isn't anyplace private enough around here for you to fuck me outdoors. We'd get our asses arrested and probably our pictures in the newspaper for public exposure!"

"No Bill! No, not here! Bill, —let's go up to the cabin for the rest of the week-end! Bill, I told Janice that I might be up there some this week-end anyway, and since somebody might have tried to call the house and I did not answer, if I'm going to use the cabin as my excuse, then I'd better go up there, at least long enough to know everything is OK up there. I'd hate to say I was there only to find out later that something funny happened up there that I would have known about if I had actually been there. Bill, it's way out by itself! Hell my cell phone don't even work out there! We can run around naked and fuck outside whenever we want! Bill, come on man, —tell me you will go! You can call Sue at her hotel and tell her we happened to see each other, and I asked if you wanted to go fishing for a day or so. You sure don't have to tell her that I am taking you up there to fuck your ass! Come on man, please!"

"Yeah, I will Jim. Yeah, let's do that! The idea of getting fucked outside is what is making me agree. God Jim! Shit man! Yesterday morning I was just some ole straight married guy that had never fucked around with some other guy before, and now, less than 24 hours later, I have not only fucked you, shot my wad in your mouth and up your ass, but you have done all of the same to me, and now I am going to get my ass fucked out, in the great out of doors!"

Then with a very big grin on his face, Bill looked at Jim and asked, "You what? You're what!? You're gonna throw me across some old log or something and then rape my ass? Shit man, I never ever thought that I'd have days like this! Jim, this is damn exciting, but man everything is it moving so fast! Do you want to finish fucking me here, or do you want to hold your cum load for up there?"

"Yeah man, yeah! Rape you across some old big log! Yeah! No, I'm not pulling out! I'll rebuild a new load. Right now the idea of doing some fucking outside in the wide open is getting me so damn excited, there is no way I can pull out of you now! Lay still, —I'm going to load your ass, and the way I'm all excited now, it will only take me about three pushes up in your ass to make my cum fly! Hang on man, I'm going to do you now!"

Jim resumed his fucking and it did take only about three or four thrusts into Bill's ass before he started yelling, "Bill, I'm cumin man, —I'm cumin! Hang on man, —I'm, —I'm cummmmmin! Oh shit man! Oh shit, why does that feel so damn good when I cum in your ass like that? Shit Bill, is it your tight ass hole that makes it feel so damn good? Shit man! I've cum for years now, but cumin has never felt that damn good until just last night and now again this morning! Bill, if that has anything to do with it, now I understand why there are as many gay guys, as there are. Shit man! I think I understand now! Bill, I think the gays have something going for them that we just did not understand! Shit man, I wish I had tried a guy a long time ago now! I've heard of some gays that try to have sex with straight guys, and now, I think that all that was going on there, was the gay guy was just trying to get the straight guy to know something! I'll never make fun of a gay guy from this time on! They know what in the hell they are doing!"

After Jim managed to re-collect himself from his complete dumping of cum, he rolled off of Bill's butt, and suggested that maybe they needed to check under the bed and see if that wooden slat was completely busted, or just cracked.

"Look's OK to me." Bill said after checking the bottom of the bed. "I'll worry about it some other time. If it's actually broken, then I'll just happen to find it, or maybe just replace it sometime when I'm here by myself. Let's take a shower and then I need to get these sheets and stuff in the wash so I can kind of put the house back the way it was before we leave."

The two men got up from off of the floor, and headed for the bathroom.

As Bill stepped into the shower, he told Jim, "Come on man. Let's shower together like we did last night. I want us to re-do the last night shower thing. I want you to feel me like you did last night and let me make believe that we are doing it for the first time again."

Bill and Jim stepped into the shower and got the water temperature adjusted. Jim grabbed the soap and started lathering Bill up.

"Yeah man! Yeah! Yeah, Jim, lather me up down under my dick. Use that soap as a reason to grab ahold of my dick and my balls and rub 'em around! Lather my legs! Get me all soapy man! I love the feel of your hands rubbing that soap on me."

Jim lathered Bill's neck, his shoulders, his back, his chest, around his waist and then knelt down on his knees to start lathering up Bill's crotch and his legs.

Suddenly Bill kind of jumped back and looked at Jim.

"Hey man! Hey, I've got to take a piss, and I want to piss on you!" Bill told Jim as all of a sudden, he started letting it flow! "I didn't take an early morning piss like you did when we woke up, so now it's my turn. I want to watch my piss flow all over you Jim. Lean in toward it man! Let it hit you in the chin. You don't have to drink it, —just let it flow over you. Yeah, lean forward. Let it run down your back. Throw your head up and let me shower your neck. Let it run down off of your tits man. Oh shit Jim! Shit that is so hot to watch! My warm piss all over your body! Jim, lean back a little and let me spray your gut so you can watch my piss flow down around your dick. Yeah, man, watch that! That's hot to me! Now, I do have to admit that I have thought before, about wanting to piss on some guy. Why I've wanted to do that in the past, I really don't know, but Jim I have wanted to watch my piss flow on some guy for years now. Why would I have wanted to do that? I've never wanted to piss on a gal, but I do admit that for some reason, I have wondered what it would be like to piss on some guy! And Jim, you are the guy that I finally got to piss on. It's OK with you that I'm doing this, right? God I hope so!"

"Hell yes it is man! Because I am going to return the favor! I need to piss again. I think the reason I need to piss again is just because the sight of me getting pissed on was so damn hot to me, that now I just have to let it flow. Bill, I hope you don't mind if I piss on you, —do you?"

"Hell no! I don't mind! Jim, stand up here and let me have it. Pee on me Jim, pee on me!"

Jim stood up and started letting his piss flow, and Bill immediately squatted down in front of Jim's crotch.

"Jim, spray my face! Jim, pee on my face!"

"Well, OK Bill, — if that's what you want! If you want it in the face, I'll be more than glad to piss on your face!"

Jim started spraying on Bill's face, and all of a sudden, Bill grabbed Jim's dick and threw his mouth on it. He started drinking Jim's piss! He pulled Jim up closer and clamped his mouth completely around Jim's cock so that he did not loose any of the warm smooth piss that Jim was now feeding him.

As Jim ran out of piss flow, Bill lovingly patted Jim's butt and said "Thanks man! Thanks! Jim I hope that did not freak you out too much, but when I told you that I had wondered for some time what it would be like to piss on some guy, well the other part of that was that I have wanted to drink some guy's piss for a long time too. My wanting to piss on him was just part of it. I kind of guess that was just to get the chance to drink from him. I really wanted to take some guy's piss down my throat. I've wanted to drink some guy's piss for a long time now! Jim, I don't know why I've wanted to do that. I never thought about fucking him or sucking on his cock or anything like that, I just wanted to see what drinking his piss would be like. Jim, I hope you are OK with me drinking your piss!"

"Hell yeah, Bill! I'm OK with that! Shit man if I had known that earlier today, I'd have fed you all of that early morning piss that I flushed down the toilet earlier. Shit man, I won't have to worry about me finding a restroom on the way to the cabin today. If I need to piss, I'll just pull over to the side of the road and let you have a drink!"

"Oh Jim, I'm glad you don't have a problem with that! Jim, ever since we came over here last night, I've been trying to get up the nerve to tell you that I wanted you to piss in my mouth and I just could not get up enough nerve to tell you. I was really afraid that you would not want to do that and maybe tell me I was crazy for wanting that. You know Jim, I kind of wonder if last night at the cafe, when I suggested we feel each other, while we jerked ourselves off, —I wonder if maybe in the back of my mind I was really hoping that this would happen. Jim, do you think maybe that is what I was really thinking and hoping when I suggested we come over here together?"

"Well hell, it probably was Bill, but don't worry about it! I'm just sorry that you were too scared to just tell me up front that you wanted to do that. Shit man, for what we have done with each other last night and today, why should one of us be afraid to tell the other one something that we want to do? I think we can be pretty straight forward with each other now, don't you?"

"Yeah, I think you are right, but maybe using the term, straight forward, is not really the right phrase for us anymore. Jim, I'm not so sure we can really claim the term straight, so much anymore. Maybe I'm wrong guy, but when I am with you, I think I really am a gay guy. Maybe I've never realized it before, but as long as I can reach out and touch you, I really don't have any problem of thinking that maybe, —yeah just maybe, —I really am a gay guy! Jim, I'm not sure a really straight guy can feel this much excitement about doing it with another guy! A lot is sure going through my mind right now, but the one thing that I know for sure is that I love being with you and having sex with you! When I was drinking your piss, —I was in heaven man! Pure heaven!"

CHAPTER SEVEN:

Headed for the Cabin

After Bill finished drinking Jim's piss, they finished showering down, of course by thoroughly soaping each other all over,— in every body cavity possible, rinsed off, dried off, and made sure they had "everything" in the wash, so that they could get the house back to its normal stance before they headed for the cabin.

With all appropriate towels, sheets, rags and anything else that had grease on them, now in the wash, the two new, "best of friends," —"best of sex friends," had some breakfast and got themselves ready for the drive up to Jim's cabin.

Bill called Sue and left a message at her hotel room that he was going fishing with Jim, and he would be back home Sunday evening.

"Man, I've got to tell you Jim. I never lie to Sue, and I have to admit that not really telling her the complete truth is making me pretty uncomfortable. I've never done anything like this before, and I'm not being real comfortable with it."

"Bill, tell you what. We'll take the fishing gear, and we'll spend at least a little time fishing, and that way, you will have been completely truthful, —you went fishing with me. OK, so yeah, —we kind of failed to mention some other stuff, like sucking and fucking, but what you did tell her is the truth!"

The men loaded the car, rechecked the house to make sure everything was back in place as if nothing had happened, and Jim turned toward Bill and said, "We are headed for the cabin!"

Jim then added, "OK! About a two hour drive, —you and me together, sitting right beside each other, and I have to keep my hands off of you for the entire drive. Don't know if that's going to work so well! You are just too damn hot to me today to think I can be that good of a guy!"

"Well Jim. Isn't there a roadside rest area up by the interstate exchange?"

"Yeah, —yes there is! And, you are thinking, —what?"

"I am thinking that if we happen to stop there, and the restroom just happens to be kind of on the empty side, then I just might need to give you a blow job to keep you under control for the rest of the drive."

"Oh my God Bill, —do you think we should do that? There in the rest stop area? Oh Bill, that's kind of exciting! Oh shit man! Getting a blow job in a roadside rest area? Got to admit, that's sure sounding like something that I have always heard the gay guys do! Bill, we sure are doing all of the gay stuff all of a sudden!"

Jim readjusted his seating position, readjusted his dick, reached over to Bill, grabbed his hand and said, "Bill, I am so damn thankful for this week-end! I am so damn glad you and I have found this new kind of a friendship. I like it!"

"I do too Jim, I do too!"

The drive continued in a very normal manner. Some very normal conversation, normal for two neighborhood guys that attend the same neighborhood meetings, and then some rather un-normal conversation between two guys that within the past day have discovered that, male to male, sex is a completely new and far more exciting experience than either one had ever imagined. And they both agreed how weird it was that neither one of them felt guilty about their new relationship and their sexual activity together.

"Hey did you see that sign Jim?"

"Yeah Bill, —I sure did. Roadside rest three miles! I've never looked forward to a roadside rest area with so much excitement and anticipation as I have been this one! I hope to hell it's not busy. Damn man, I hope that restroom is empty!"

The three miles quickly disappeared and Jim turned into the rest area. Both men silently, but with excited anticipation, got out of the car. Walking side by side, they approached the restroom. A father and his son came out just as they approached. They entered. They checked out the room and each of the stalls.

Quietly Bill said. "Nobody's here Jim. It's just you and me!"

"Bill, where should we do this? Out here in the open? Should we go in one of the stalls?"

"Yeah, Jim. Yeah, let's go in here! If we think anybody is coming in we can just be real quiet and not let them know two guys are in here."

Bill and Jim entered the stall up against the side wall. Jim turned toward Bill and immediately dropped his cut off shorts. He wore no underwear. His cock immediately flew out, completely hard and at attention.

Bill knelt down and grabbed it with his left hand. He drew it up toward his mouth. He placed it in his mouth and started sucking. He grabbed Jim's hips and pulled Jim closer to himself. He pushed and pulled on Jim's torso so that he could create a lot of body action into and out of his mouth, as he enjoyed Jim's rod pushing on the back of his throat.

"Bill, somebody just came in." Jim very quietly said.

Bill got very quiet. Neither man moved.

They stood still for about a minute and heard someone flush a urinal. They then heard the water running in a lavatory, a paper towel dispenser being used, and then silence.

"They're gone." Jim said.

Bill resumed his sucking and grabbing onto Jim's body.

Suddenly Jim said, "Bill, somebody closed that door! Bill, I hear a lock."

"OK guys, open the stall door! This is the park ranger! Open the door!" All of a sudden Jim and Bill realized they were not the only men in the restroom, as they had thought! "Open the door men!"

Bill stood up, Jim grabbed his cut offs and Jim unlocked the stall door.

"Good! Thanks!" The ranger said as Jim opened the stall door.

Jim and Bill looked out of the stall and saw a state park trooper standing immediately outside of the stall and looking very sternly as he looked Jim and Bill over.

"So just what in the hell do you two guys think you are doing in here? This is not a bathhouse! This is a state roadside rest area! A public restroom, —not a public sex room!

The trooper looked to be in his very early thirties, about 6 foot one, probably about 190 pounds and from the way his uniform fit, in one hell of a good physical shape.

The appearance of this hot looking specimen did not go unnoticed by Bill or Jim. Both men quickly wondered to himself of just why he was so damn quick to notice how hot, —in his mind anyway, —this state park ranger was. Each of the two wondered just why this hot looking man was so noticeable to him, now, on this day, when at any other time, his appearance would not have been of any notice to him.

"I've locked the door. I've put a sign out front that this restroom is closed. When we have this kind of a problem, we have found out it's best to just have some nice private time in here without others coming in. So it's just you two and me. And you are locked in. So don't either one of you think you can just get out of here! So just what in the hell did you two think you were up to? This is not a public sex place! It's a state roadside rest facility, remember!?"

"OK, OK men. One of you start talking and one of you tell me just what in the hell was going on! One of you was getting sucked off. Right?"

The ranger then looked at Bill and asked the same question again. "Well, —was one of you getting sucked off? Were you the one getting sucked off?"

Bill answered very softly and quietly, "Yeah, —yes I was getting sucked off."

The ranger then immediately looked at Jim and said, "Oh, so you are the sucker here? You like to suck, right?" The ranger asked. "You like cock, —right?" Then looking at Bill he continued, "Hey, show me what he was sucking on. Let me see what he had in his mouth!"

Bill dropped his shorts only to his knees and let his cock be exposed.

The ranger looked at it and said, "Well, at least he knows how to find a good looking cock when he wants to suck on one, don't he?" Then looking directly at Bill asked, "You suck cock too?"

Bill replied, "Well, —I've sucked him, —but he's the only one I've ever sucked on. Yesterday was the first time I ever did that."

"What!? What!?" The ranger exclaimed. "Yesterday, you mean like, —yesterday? Yesterday was the first time you ever sucked your buddy here?"

"Yeah, yeah!" Bill replied. "Yeah, yesterday was the first time either one of us ever did anything like that. We're straight guys. We're not gay."

"Yeah! Yeah, —right!" The ranger almost yelled. "Yeah, right! Two guys that suck on each other, and probably fuck each other, —right? But, no, —oh no, —I'm not gay! Just straight guys, playing with each other's dicks and asses, just like they are gay guys! Yeah, —right! Sure have heard that a few times in the past. Oh, —but I'm straight! Yeah, right!"

Jim and Bill quietly stood there listening to the ranger exclaim about how, —yeah, —they are sucking and fucking each other, but they are not gay! Neither man had a good comeback! They each simply stood there and looked at him.

"Interesting! Interesting!" The ranger said as he checked out the hands on each guy. "Wedding rings on each of you! Is that wedding rings between the two of you, to each other, or are those representing some little ole women in your lives?"

"Yeah, —women." Jim said.

"Oh! Oh, how great this is!" The ranger replied. "Two guys drive in here together, go suck each other off in the restroom, and they each have a woman at home thinking they are the only wives you each have, when in reality, you are fucking each other, right? A female wife and a male wife, —both?"

"Well, like we said, yesterday was the very first time for either of us. Before that, neither one of us ever thought about doing it with a guy. Yesterday it just happened."

"You know guys," the ranger said. "You know, the reason I know you two drove in here together is because we are constantly on the watch out for guys like you. Well, kind of like you. Ones that come out here to use our place when they need to get together with another guy. The reason we lock them in is so we can completely explain just what kind of legal trouble they are going to be in if they are caught again. We keep track of who we talk to in here. We throw them back out as soon as we get their attention and, of course, get their names and addresses, but you know guys, you are a little different. Different in that you came in here together. That must mean something. I'm not sure just what, but it is different. Usually the guys come from different places. You two are traveling together, and the main thing is, I actually do kind of believe you that yesterday was your very first time. The way you are both acting, I kind of believe it. I do think you are both nice married hubbies, and somehow you managed to find out yesterday what good sex was all about. Guys, I have never done this before, I don't want to jeopardize my job, but since the door is locked, and nobody can come in, and you two are the hottest looking guys I've found in here for a hell of a long time, I want some action from the two of you, too! You two really are the hottest looking guys I've locked in here ever since I started this job, and I want to enjoy you guys. You let me have some good fun with you two and I will not even find out what your names are, and there will be no record of you ever being in here. OK?"

The ranger started rubbing his expanding crotch, looked at each man, and then said, "Well men, I've made you a proposal. Want it, —or do I take your names and addresses? Remember, you have wives back there!"

"Yeah, —we want it!" Bill said. "Yeah we want it! Say yes Jim! Tell him yes, we do want it. We will do the sex thing!"

Jim looked at Bill, then looked at the ranger and said, "Yeah, —yes we do. Let's suck!"

The ranger grinned largely and said, "OK guys, let's get naked. This is going to be good. And, if you guys have truly only done this since yesterday, maybe I can teach you each something."

"Hey guys! The ranger thing, —and the two "bad" guys, —deal, is over! I'm wanting the sex stuff and so from now on it's just three guys having fun together. OK? Just three guys, that just happen to be in a nice safe locked place, doing each other! OK?"

Jim and Bill looked at the ranger and with a smile on each of their faces, they each replied, "Yeah, —OK. Yeah, sounds good!"

"Hey men, if we are going to be enjoying each other's bodies, I think we should know what to call each other. I'm Tom." The ranger told them, as he stripped out of his clothes.

"I'm Bill." Bill replied as he shook hands with Tom.

"I'm Jim." Jim replied and also shook hands.

"OK guys." Tom said. "What activities have you two done so far? What have you discovered?"

Bill and Jim rather quickly detailed to Tom just what had happened between the two of them, and explained what actions they have been involved in so far.

"Oh OK!" Tom said. "Sounds pretty normal, except yeah, I will say it does sound kind of like you two really went into finding out as much as you could, as quickly as you could. Got to admit! Drinking some other guy's piss on the first day is pretty abnormal. I can tell you two have really been ready for this, —you just never knew it!"

"Since I kind of guess we are at my place, as bare of a place as it might be, I guess it is still kind of my home ground, so I'm going to take the lead here and kind of get stuff going. Is that OK with you two guys?" Tom asked.

"Yeah, sure is with me." Jim answered. "Tom, you've got to understand that Bill and I are still really very new to this whole thing, and of course neither one of us has ever been with two guys at the same time before. I guess, you'd call that a, three-way, right?"

"Yeah, right man! It's a three way! And to get it going, Jim you get back on Bill's dick, like I guess you were before I interrupted you guys earlier. You suck him, and I'm going to get down under you and start doing some licking and sucking on you."

Jim bent over and took Bill's cock into his mouth. Bill leaned back against the wall and offered all of his meat rod to his friend. Bill grabbed ahold of Jim's head and pulled him forward.

Tom knelt down on the floor and placed his head up under Jim's crotch. He took Jim's bag into his mouth. He rolled Jim's balls around inside of his mouth, and then clamping some onto the bag sack, he pulled on the bag. He heard Jim groan, but not a bad groan. It was a pleasant groan. He pulled more. Another slight groan. He again rolled Jim's balls around inside of his mouth! He felt Jim move his body back toward himself, as if to offer his bag to Tom, for Tom to enjoy!

As Tom chewed on Jim's bag, he could feel the movement of Jim taking advantage of Bill's hungry mouth. He liked and enjoyed the movement of Jim's body above his face. He allowed Jim's bag to pop out of his mouth. Tom moved his mouth back toward Jim's butt cheeks. He repositioned himself so that his face was very nicely placed right at the lower side of Jim's butt. He looked up, and moved his nose right in between Jim's butt cheeks.

Jim remembered the excitement that he had the night before when Bill had placed his tongue up between his tight butt cheeks.

Jim exclaimed with excitement, "Oh Tom, lick my ass please! Oh Tom, can you lick my ass please!?"

Tom immediately took the request. He did not hesitate. He grabbed each side of Jim's ass and pulled it apart. He immediately rammed his face up into Jim's ass as far as he possibly could. He pushed on Jim's ass so strongly that Jim force fucked Bill's mouth without having any control over how hard he was ramming his mouth. Bill was choking. He had to push Jim back away from his mouth. He needed to take a deep breath.

Tom grabbed Jim's hip line and forced his face as far forward as he could. He extended his tongue and feverishly started licking as far inside of Jim's ass muscles as he could. He again grabbed Jim's ass cheeks and pulled them as far apart as possible.

He pulled his face out from the muscled confines and without even realizing what he was saying, he exclaimed, "Oh man! Oh man! I want to tongue fuck your tight ass! Oh man! I want to tongue fuck you!"

Immediately he forced his face back in the ass crack. He stretched his tongue out as far as possible. All of a sudden his tongue felt the small round shrunken closed hole that he was so hungry for. He slid the tip of his tongue in. He slid it around in circles in an attempt to slightly open the tightly closed asshole. He felt it so very slightly open. He pushed with all of the face force, he could find, to get more of his tongue up and in Jim's ass.

Jim was attempting to face fuck Bill at the same time that he was getting tongue fucked himself. He told Tom, "Tom, let me lay down on the floor and try to relax my ass muscles more so that you can get up in there, OK?"

Tom pulled back and said, "Yeah Jim. Yeah. Here, throw these clothes on the floor and use them under you. Lay down here and let me at it!"

Jim pulled off of Bill's rod and laid down on the floor. Tom immediately laid down on Jim and placed his mouth right at Jim's ass. Grabbing each cheek, he pulled the butt muscles apart and slammed his face into Jim's ass. He licked excitedly the inside edges of Jim's butt. He pulled the cheeks apart afar as he could and he went for the asshole. He extended his tongue out as far as he could, and entered Jim's ass. He rolled his tongue around and completely enjoyed the smell of Jim's ass, and the taste of the inside of his ass. He pushed his face in even farther. He licked the moisture with his tongue and inhaled through his nose. The aroma of Jim's ass made him inhale more often than what was actually necessary! He could feel his tongue flip the edges of Jim's ass hole. Jim could feel his asshole flipping also. Jim moaned and groaned a very pleasant and excited groan.

Jim rather moaned and then almost yelled, "Yeah man! Yeah! Oh yeah, that feels good in my ass! Lick my ass! Lick me inside and out! Lick me! Oh yeah man! Get your lips on my asshole and blow air up in me. Blow my butt! Yeah, blow air up in my ass! Oh yeah, that feels so good to me. Yeah, lick my hole!"

Bill started feeling kind of left out once Tom got himself squarely positioned on top of Jim's ass and was eating it out so completely. Bill decided that he needed to be involved too. He looked down and realized that, maybe without actually realizing it, Tom was definitely offering his own asshole for some good invasions too.

Bill hit the floor, stretched out, belly down, and placed his face right at the muscular structure of Tom's ass. He grabbed Tom's torso and immediately threw his head down into the crevice of Tom's hot, and hungry ass. He grabbed Tom's ass cheeks and pulled them apart. He extended his tongue out as far as possible and reached it toward the small little hole that he knew was hidden in between those butt cheeks. As he pulled on the cheek muscles, he forced his head down as far as he could and with his tongue sticking out and begging as forcefully as it could, he found the opening that he had suddenly gotten so excited about invading. The hole he had never see before or even touched before, but the hole that he was now terribly anxious to lick dry!

Bill curled his tongue and pushed it in the hole. He took a deep breath through his nose. As he smelt Tom's ass, he liked what he smelt! He took another deep breath! He rolled his tongue around with all of the might that he could muster. He rammed his head forward and forced Tom's cheeks to allow him further entry! He was now actually licking the inside of Tom's ass and he was in glory! He liked what he was doing! Suddenly he re-lived the ass licking experience that he had just so recently experienced, when he licked the inside of Jim's ass the night before.

Twice within only one day, Bill had been face up, in a guy's asshole, licking in it as deep as he could reach. Once again he started to realize that he was having more unexplained excitement doing this with a guy, even a guy he did not know, than he had ever experienced in having straight sex. He felt his heart pump! He rammed his face back into Tom's ass as far as he could go! He licked! He ran his tongue around in circles and rammed it into the tinny hole as far as he could force it. Once he had it in as far as he could reach, he laid still and enjoyed the excitement of knowing that his tongue, well, —as much of it as he could get in, was up inside of Tom's ass, and he was excited about it. He was tongue fucking some guy that he actually did not even know. He did not know if this Tom guy was some straight guy, maybe he was a married guy too, or maybe he was a gay guy that has a partner that either tongues this ass every night, or maybe fucks this ass with his big rod every night. Bill was getting himself very excited with just the pondering of who, and what this other guy was. He was having some very exciting sex with some guy that he knew nothing about, and he was finding that sex, more exciting than he thought was possible! Anonymous sex! Sucking and licking on some guy's ass, some guy that he will probably never, ever see again! Wow! Something that he had never thought about before.

He kept wondering about what normal activity usually happens back here in this guy's asshole, the same asshole that he was now so excitedly licking, —as thoroughly as he possibly could anyway!

All of a sudden, as Bill laid there completely still and tremendously enjoying the warm moist skin of Tom's ass cheeks against the front and the sides of his face, he realized nobody was moving. Bill was on top. His face was completely buried in Tom's ass. Tom was in the middle, his face was completely buried in Jim's ass. Both Tom and Bill were struggling to gain whatever small amount of air they could, by breathing through their noses, and forcing in whatever air they could gain.

Suddenly, Bill could tell that Tom was swinging his face back and forth in Jim's ass, and Bill joined the action. He too started swinging his face back and forth between Tom's ass cheeks, as much, and as fast, as he could.

As the two, face pushing, ass licking, guys finished their fun of slapping their faces back and forth within the confines of their bottom guys' asses, Jim said, "Hey guys! I've got a suggestion. Tom we're headed for the family cabin up at the lake. If we tell you how to find it, can you join us there? We're going to be there tonight and tomorrow morning and afternoon, is there anyway that you can come meet us?"

"Yeah! Hell yes I can! Yes I can!" Tom almost busted out yelling. "Hell yes guys, I can!"

Then a little more calmly he continued. "Hey guys I can't leave here till four o'clock this afternoon, but I sure can come on up then if I can. I don't have to be here tomorrow, so can I stay with you guys overnight?"

"Yeah, —yes you can." Jim replied. "Well, that is if you plan on sucking on my ass some more like you just did. And, —you've got to do Bill's ass too. I want him to see what that sucking on and blowing air up in his ass feels like!"

With the new plans in the workings, all three guys got up from on the cold and hard concrete floor and proceeded to organize just how they would handle the getting together. Jim gave Tom complete and detailed descriptions on how to find the cabin, and they figured out just what time Tom would be able to get there.

Once again checking with Tom to make sure for the second or third time that he knew how to find the cabin, Jim and Bill waited for Tom to unlock the restroom, check outside to make sure nobody saw all three of them coming out of a locked restroom, and they then headed for their car.

Just as they opened the car and started to get in, they both looked back toward the restroom area and waved to Tom. "Later man!" They each called to Tom as he waved back.

Tom yelled, "Yeah, later men! Drive safely!"

As Jim and Bill headed out to finish their drive, Jim asked Bill, "Hey. I didn't ask you before I invited him to come up and join us. I hope that's OK with you. You don't mind that I just did that without checking with you first, do you?"

"Shit, hell no!" Bill quickly responded. "Shit man! I kinda think I have a feeling that having him up there is going to make the rest of this week-end even that much more exciting! After the way you were acting when he had his face in your ass and as excited as you got, I'm getting really anxious to have him slam his face up in my butt and blow some air up in me to suck back out. Shit man, I sure hope he wasn't shitting us about wanting to come up and join us!"

"No Bill. I really don't think he was. I think he wants to play with us as much as we want to play with him. He's a pretty hot looking guy, isn't he?"

"Yeah Jim, he is hot looking, and did you notice that dick he was swinging back there. Neither one of us got to it, but from the looks of it, I think it is real ready and anxious to get rammed up in some guy's ass from as hard and as stiff as it was. Shit man,

I'm so damn horny right now, I can't hardly stand it! Jim, I need sex! I need sex badly!"

"Well Bill, we are only about half an hour from the turn off to the cabin, and once we get there, it's all just forest road and very private going all the way to the cabin, so if you just can't hold your anxiety any longer, when we get there, then we'll just get out, go in the woods and fuck your brains out for awhile. OK?"

"Yeah Jim! Yeah!" Bill said with a big deep breath between each word. "That's what we came up here for! Sex out in the wild! So man, don't tease me unless you mean what you're saying! I want you to throw me across some old log and fuck the hell out of me! I want to be able to yell, 'fuck me, fuck me', out as loud as I can. Jim, you had better find us some good ole deserted place! Someplace where nobody else is! We are going to be out in the wild, and I want wild, crazy, sex with you while we are out there! I want you to get blisters on your dick, —just from fucking my ass!"

CHAPTER EIGHT:

The Hill Top Meeting

"Here comes our first turn-off, Bill. We use this road for about four miles, and then we turn off onto the, what I call the "road from hell." When we get on that road, then we've got about five miles of nothing but a slow, rut filled road. The cabin is not exactly, what I would call, right on the main road, and in-fact, even that bad road stops at the cabin. The state has never done anything to fix up that old road, and so our old cabin is still the only place back there. When Grandpa and Grandma built the place, they actually used horse and wagon to get supplies back there, and they lived there all year round, seldom came out, so back then there really wasn't any need for a road. I sure have not encouraged any improvements on it since I know that if they fix it up, then others will want to build cabins back there too, and I just hope they don't. So anyway, buddy, anytime we turn off onto that old road, whenever you see a spot where you think we should stop and use to do some ole Billy butt fucking, you let me know. After that turn-off, it's just going to be me and you until Tom gets up here, so it's going to be, —fuck you crazy, out in the open, time."

The two continued the additional four miles on the more useable road, and as they turned off onto the rut-filled, old, road, Bill said. "Hey Jim, that road we just turned off of was pretty well deserted itself, I can't imagine how deserted it must be down this road. You guys sure don't come up here to the cabin very often right after it rains, I guess. Right?"

"No, we sure don't. Kind of makes the driving a little too rough!"

Slowly Bill and Jim proceeded down the very private and deserted road just about two miles. Jim slowed to a complete crawl and told Bill, this is our spot. This is where I am going to fuck your ass out in the wide open for the first go at it. If we go up that hill a little ways over there, we will be above the trees and then we will be able to look back toward the highway and we can make believe that everybody on the highway can see you getting your tight assed butt fucked!"

"Oh shit man!" Bill responded. "I know damned well we are way too far from the highway for anybody to see us, but just the idea of being out here in the wide open, getting my ass fucked and being able to watch cars drive down the highway is exciting. I guess I'll kind of imagine that somebody down there does have a strong enough pair of binoculars that they could see me getting it in the ass. Jim, everything we are doing is just plain ass exciting to me. I love this! Jim, wanting to get it out here in the open, and liking the idea that I can watch the traffic on the highway drive by while I am getting fucked, does that mean I'm an exhibitionist?"

As Jim turned into a deserted lane, that actually went nowhere, but it did get his car off of the roadway he looked at Bill and said, "Well, I don't know man, but if you are, then I guess I must be too since I am all excited about fucking your ass out here in the open, and kind of wishing somebody from the highway could watch me do it!"

The two men got out and headed up the side of the hill. Suddenly Jim stopped turned to Bill and said, "Hey wait a minute guy! How in the hell am I going to fuck your ass without some kind of grease? I think maybe I had better get that Crisco out of the food box and take it with us, unless your ass is so damn hungry that it's open so wide, I don't need any."

"Hey it's hungry for your dick, but I do think using some grease back in there is a pretty good idea. Let's get some and put it in one of the paper cups we brought, OK?"

"Yeah good idea Bill. Then I don't have to take the whole can, we can just take part of it."

The men returned the short distance back to the car, got the Crisco, put some in a paper cup and headed back up toward the top of the hill where they intended to let nature take its course, out in nature.

"Oh shit Jim! Oh yeah man! I see what you mean! This is the perfect spot. Damn I am so excited!"

Both men stripped off all of his clothes, threw them over to the side, stood tall and straight and looked down toward the highway.

"Shit Jim, this is great! Jim, I've never been out in the open totally naked, butt sticking out and my dick hanging free in the breeze like this before. Just imagine all of those people down there on the highway looking this way, and if they only realized that if they were using some good binoculars they could see you and me standing here completely naked, head to toe and with our dicks pointing straight out toward them. God Jim, this is great! Jim, I'm getting perverted, but shit man, I love it!"

Jim took the lead and he spread his feet apart, raised his hands up in the air, and said, "World, here I am! It's me, all of me, totally naked for all of you to see!"

Bill glanced over at him, took the same strutting position and said, "And me too world! Me, my body and the all of me!"

After their fun of displaying themselves to the world, as if anybody could see them, Jim then told Bill, "Well man. We did not stop here just to let the breezes blow through our crotches. Face the highway, and get down on you hands and knees. You are about to find out just what it is like to get fucked out in the great out of doors!"

And with that instruction, Bill immediately took the required position and Jim smeared some grease on his ass hole. Jokingly Jim then yelled, "Me Tarzan!" and immediately sank his rod down and into Bill's ass.

Bill jerked slightly since Jim took his ass without so much as a "get ready" statement, and without so much as a slight pause once the tip of his cock went in. It was man to man fucking the outdoors way. Fucking now and fucking heavy!! He was not in a bedroom and not on a soft bed, and he did not intend to fuck Bill's ass like they were at home in the comforts of the living room or bedroom. This was sex out in the wild, and he intended to let it be wild!

"Are you doing OK man?" Jim asked of Bill, once he had totally dominated his ass.

Bill managed a slight "Yeah, I'm OK," and Jim could tell from the slight response that Bill was feeling the effects of the wild outdoors fucking that he was trying to deliver.

"Bill my baby! Your butt is so damn good! What did you tell me earlier that you wanted to yell out here as loud as you could once we started? What did you tell me? Tell me man! I want to hear it! Let me hear it!"

"Fuck me! Fuck me!" Bill yelled out as loud as he possibly could. Then he repeated his yell, "Fuck me! Fuck me!"

"Yeah man! Yeah that is my Bill. How does it feel to yell that out as loud as you can? Does that feel good? You wanted to do that last night and this morning didn't you? You have wanted to yell, 'fuck me— fuck me', ever since we started this haven't you man!?"

Jim took ahold of Bills waist line and rammed his ass. "I'm fucking you! I'm fucking you man!" Jim yelled out at the top of his lungs. "I'm fucking you! I'm fucking you man!" He repeated.

Jim was in complete glory fucking the ass of his new buddy.

Bill was way beyond excitement getting fucked outside, in the open, in nature, the way he had now decided true sex was meant to happen.

Without so much yelling this time, Bill pleaded with Jim to fuck him good and to fuck him hard. "Yeah man! Please fuck me, please fuck me! Oh Jim, I've never felt so good. Jim, I never in the world ever thought I'd be getting fucked in the ass and I sure as hell never thought I'd be having sex outdoors like this, but oh shit man, —this is great! I'm actually getting my ass fucked outside! Oh fuck me man!"

"I am Bill, and I am about to give you a complete load. I agree, this outside stuff is way too exciting! Man oh man! I never dreamt that I'd be fucking some guy's ass let alone up on top of a hill where I could watch traffic on the highway as I fucked him. Oh! Bill I am about to cum. Bill—I'm getting close. Bill, I'm about to let you have it man! Bill, squeeze my dick with your ass man! I'm cummmmmmmin man! I'm cummmin!"

Jim pushed his dick up in Bill as far and as hard as he could and then completely locked the two bodies together as he emptied every drop as deep into Bill as he could. As he finished his explosion of cum shots, Jim laid down over the back of Bill and took in about four or five big deep breaths of air.

"Uhh guys! Uhhh guys!" Somebody said, from a small distance away.

Jim immediately pulled his stiff rod out of Bill and Bill immediately jumped up.

"Oh shit!" Jim loudly exclaimed.

"Oh God!" Bill almost yelled as he turned to see where the voice had come from, and attempted to grab his shorts at the same time.

"Hey guys, —no problem! Everything's OK!" The voice said in a comforting tone. "Everything's OK. Don't panic men, everything's OK!"

The person with the mysterious voice came into view from the confines of the closest trees. "Don't panic men. I do that with my buddies all the time. Everything's OK!"

Bill and Jim continued to re-dress themselves and looked at and toward the person approaching their area.

Seriously guys, there's no problem. Well, anyway not with what is going on here. Guys, I am a gay guy too, so don't worry. The problem is, —I'm stuck out here in the forest with no transportation. Hey guys, I work for the Forest Service and my truck broke down and I am stuck out here with no way back to the station. I need your help if I can, please."

"How long have you been there?" Bill asked.

"Well, long enough to see what was happening, and long enough to be jealous of what was happening. I was down on the road, and I found your car but I did not know where you were until I heard the yelling. And of course when I heard the yelling that I did, then I really did want to find you. Thank goodness you guys yell when you are fucking each other or I would not have known which direction to go." And with a big grin on his face the Forest worker said, "Oh, —you guys yell good, —too! What a way to meet someone! I guess I could call this, what, —a hill top meeting? What a trip men!"

Jim and Bill got themselves all rather re-gathered together and asked the Forest worker just what had happened to his truck, and they told him they were damn thankful that it was a gay guy that heard them, since they had been completely convinced that there was nobody, absolutely nobody, within hearing distance when they yelled out!

The Forest worker explained that the Superintendent wanted to borrow his long-bed pick-up, so that some other workers could take some construction material up to the Upper Cliff Look-out area, and had given him the old truck to use for a couple of days.

"This old truck is kind of a backup for us, and since I was going to have to use it for a couple of days, the Superintendent told me that I'd just do some routine maintenance checks and not have to take the truck off of the road. Well hell! The damn radio in it worked the first time I used it, and then after that, it's dead. I can't get it to do anything, and of course, I did not check to make sure it had a good spare in it, which it did not! I got a flat, and the damn spare is as completely flat as the one that was on the road! The truck is about a mile on down the road, and I was on my way out to the other road, hoping somebody would come by. I knew damn well nobody would be on this back road, and when I found your car parked down there, I was really surprised. Then when I heard the yelling, hell man—I got all excited! And I got to admit, I got all excited for more than just finding someone! Can you guys help me out any? Are you guys heading in, or are you headed back out to the main road?"

"We're headed in." Jim replied. "We're headed in to my cabin."

'The cabin!? You are headed into the old cabin at the end of the road?" The Forest worker asked.

"Yeah, my family owns that cabin, and we are headed back there for the rest of the week-end. We are not going back out till tomorrow, later afternoon, but if want to wait until then, we can take you back out or to wherever you need to go then."

"Yeah we could do that!" Bill chipped in. "Hi, I'm Bill, and this is Jim."

"Oh, Hi guys. I'm Brian."

The two city guys shook hands with Brian and expressed their pleasure of meeting him.

"Brian, if you want to hang out with us for the night, we can help you tomorrow, but we've got another guy headed this way to meet up with us, and if we're not at the cabin when he gets there, I'm afraid that he'll think he went to the wrong place. We need to go to the cabin, and we really don't have enough time to take you back to town, right now."

"If you guys don't mind, I'd like to spend the night with you guys. I'll worry about my damn truck problems tomorrow. When we go out on checks like this anyway, we always take overnight stuff with us and spend the night out in the forest, so nobody is going to know anything is wrong until I don't show up by about sunset tomorrow anyway, so I'd like to stay with you guys. I've got stuff in my truck, some grub that I had with me, and my sleeping bag and clothes, that I'd like to stop and get since we will be going past the truck on the way in anyway, if I could."

"No problem, if your truck is up the road, which I guess of course it is or we would have seen it when we came in." Jim said.

"Uhh, hey guys." Brian said. "The other guy that is coming up to the cabin later, is he gay too?"

Jim looked at Bill, Bill looked at Jim, both looked puzzled and Jim said, "Brian, we really don't know. We assume so, but really, we don't know. See, we aren't gay either. We are just friends that know each other from living in the same neighborhood."

"Wait—Wait!" Brian quickly said as he looked at Jim and then at Bill. "Wait guys! Wait here a minute! I am the same guy that was in the trees, —you were on your hands and knees with your butt up in the air, —you were straddling his butt with your cock rammed all the way up in his ass, —you were yelling 'Fuck me! Fuck me man!,' and you were yelling, 'I'm fucking you! I'm fucking you man,' and now you are telling me you guys are not gay. I'm the same guy that was watching you fuck him for all your might, and I'm the same guy that watched him fuck you with all his might!! What in the hell does it take to be a gay guy! Hey men—I really do kind of think you both hit the description right on the head, —no pun intended there guys!"

Bill looked at Jim and kind of shook his head. Jim looked at Bill and kind of shook his head.

"Brian, come on." Bill said. "Let's head for the car and we will tell you why we said that. You might be right, but right now we are kind of confused on that issue. We'll fill you in, and hell, maybe you might be able to help us figure ourselves out."

The three men walked down the hill and got to the car. On the way back to the car, Bill and Jim had a little time to start explaining the past day. They filled Brian in on all of the activities that they had personally discovered between themselves, and explained the situation with Tom.

"Tom, that's the same Tom that works for the state over at the roadside rest area? The tall guy that looks like he has the body of death on him?" Brian asked.

"Yeah!" Jim said. "You know him?"

"Hell yes, I know him!" Brian answered. "Shit yes. Every gay guy this side of the Mississippi knows that one. Hell yes! I have seen him at the 'Go There or Go Square' bar a lot of times, but he is always so ganged up on by all of the hunky guys, I've never gotten to meet him directly or,— as we like to say, up close and up tight!"

"Well shit Brian! What do you mean by all of the hunky guys! What in the hell do you think you are? You are what, —like maybe 23, 5 feet 11, 175 or 180, what about a 44 chest and a 30 or 31 inch waist? Brian, how close am I?" Bill asked as he looked the younger man up and down as he sat in the back seat of the car.

"Damn man! Shit man! You must have a hell of a lot experience in checking out guys. Shit you are even right on with my age! Crap man! How in the hell do you do that? The only thing that you were not quite right on was the chest and waist. Last time I measured, my chest was 45 and a half, and my waist was 32 and a half. Shit man, you are so good, tell me what size dick I've got, even though you haven't yet seen it! How long am I?"

"Hey, now this is getting tricky. Pull it out, and then I'll guess! OK?'

"No, no man! Got to wait till later! I'll let you find out up real, real close, but you've got to wait till we get to the cabin. Then it's back to naked time, and back to some more yelling out in the woods. Do I get to yell, Fuck me, —fuck me, or do I get to yell, I'm fucking you! I'm fucking you man?"

Being careful to avoid all of the deep ruts in the road, Jim had not been in the conversation, but with that question, he did enter, "Hey man. If your body is as hot as I think it is, you get to yell both, since you will be fucking one of us and getting fucked by the other one, and all at the same time!"

And then looking over at Bill, he continued, "And the way Tom likes to use his tongue, I kind of guess he will be the one on the very back-end, doing his 'Tom tongue' thing, as deeply as he can."

"His 'Tom tongue', thing?" Brian asked. "His 'Tom tongue' thing? What are you meaning. Are there activities about Tom that I have never heard about? 'Tom tongue'? Do you mean what I am assuming you are saying?"

Bill turned toward Brian and grinning, replied, "Yeah Brian, you are assuming right! If you have known Tom around before, but have never had the chance to do stuff with him, if you like your ass licked and sucked on, tonight you are going to get a chance to get to know the real Tom and his, —as we call it, —'Tom tongue' thing! He did Jim at the roadside rest today, and he promised that I get it tonight, so I guess maybe we will just form a line and let ole Tom work his way from butt hole to butt hole! And let me tell you! The way he went to Jim's ass today, I'm sure that he would be happy and excited if we had fifty guys all lined up for him tonight!"

"Listen to that guy talk!" Jim entered. "Shit man! Sir Bill, I think you must be forgetting that while he had his face rammed up in my ass, you were doing a pretty good job up in his ass too! I'm not so sure we can say Tom is the only tongue user here. Your tongue was pretty active back there too!"

After the rather slow and careful drive the rest of the way to the cabin, they finally reached the edge of the property and Jim pulled the car into the driveway. As they opened the doors, each man got out, and without even telling the other two of what he was doing, immediately removed all of his cloths. All three looked at each other in complete shock that the other two had done the same thing, without anybody admitting that was going to be his first move, once out of the car."

"Damn, —shit Jim!" Bill exclaimed. "Look at that damn big rod on that guy! Holy shit man! I guess they must be passing out bigger dicks now, than they were back when I was born! Crap man! Look at the size of that thing!"

Jim looked at Brian's mammoth rod, took a deep breath, then looked over at Bill and said, "Bill, wipe the slobbers off of the side of your mouth! You are drooling, man!"

CHAPTER NINE:

North Point Sanctuary

The three each gathered up the clothes he had quickly gotten out of, as Bill said, "Oh shit man! This is great! I did not know I was a nudist in nature, but now that I am out in nature, I sure do admit now, that I am a nudist in nature. This feels so damn good to just let it all hang out and swing any damn way it wants to. I never realized I actually wanted to just run around in front of other guys, all bare assed. This is fun! I'll be glad when Tom gets here too. Then I'll be the naked, wild animal, in front of three other guys. Hell, the way I feel right now, I guess I really would not care if this place had a whole bunch of people here. All of a sudden, I feel like clothes are a real un-necessary!"

"I agree!" Jim replied. "I never knew running around naked is so damn exciting. Whenever I'm up here the family is always with me, but even if I had been here by myself, I'm not so sure that I would have gotten into the idea of getting bare assed naked and just letting the wind blow through. Brian, do you, or have you, gone naked out in the wilds before?"

"Yeah guys! All the time, —well as often as possible. I kind of think that is one of the main reasons a lot of guys become Forest Rangers. It gives us the chance to strip it all off and just be good and naked outside. Like I told you earlier, when we go out on these maintenance checks, we always take overnight stuff with us, and really I think that kind of got started just because the guys all realized that was their best chance of doing the bare assed thing. We get away from people as soon as possible, and then strip it all off! I know there are four of us, —out of just my section anyway, that do it, and as often as possible! Whenever we have to pair up for an overnight, we always try to get paired up with one of the guys that likes to hang it naked. Then we know we can do it, and nobody cares."

"The other guys from your section that like to do it, are they gay guys that like to fool around when you're running around naked?" Jim inquired.

"Two of them play around. One is definitely gay, and available to anybody, one of them is 'bi', I guess I'd say. Well anyway, I kind of think maybe we made him, 'bi'! He's a black man and originally he wouldn't do anything at all, even though he might be there just watching a couple of us going to it, but then a couple of years ago, he got kind of involved one night, so now he plays, but he is very, very secretive about it. He's got a family and he sure does not want anybody to know what he is up to. Kind of like you two, I guess!"

Then there is Jack, and he is straight, but that is OK with the rest of us guys. He knows we play around, but we don't play in front of him. We tell him that's because we respect him, but really, he's not the kind of a guy you would like to take home at night. Nice guy, but just not the kind you really want to play with. Too straight laced and not too much of a body either. So anyway, we just don't do anything that would make him change his mind. I think he does most of his overnights by himself, where the rest of us always try to have a reason that at least two of us need to go out together. Shit man, one night, —oh hell, —I've got to tell you about that night! It was just about two years ago and Sam, the other openly gay guy, and I were on an overnighter. This was before Todd, the married guy ever did any playing around stuff with us. Well, as things turned out, this was his first time."

"Sam and I were up by what is called the North Point Sanctuary and we were all alone, or so we thought! It was toward sunset, and we had been playing around with each other and there were two couples in the area that we did not know were there. They were older, bird watching, people. Obviously very quiet, and one of them, I think it was one of the men, saw us playing around. Thankfully we did not have any uniforms on, so they didn't know we were rangers. They headed out of there without letting us know we had been seen, but they stopped at the Ranger Station and reported what he had seen. The ranger at the station right then, just thank goodness, was Todd. He told those people that he would go up and get rid of whoever it was that they had seen. He was pretty sure it was us, but of course he never mentioned that to anybody. When the people headed out toward the highway, he headed up for the sanctuary. He wanted those people to know he was definitely doing something about what was happening. Well anyway, when he got up here and found us, we were still going at it, or going at it again, anyway. Sam was fucking the hell out of my ass, and Todd stood there for what he said was probably four or five minutes and watched us before we knew he was anywhere around. He told us that although he knew we did that kind of stuff together, he had never really watched it happen with any intent before, and this time it made him get a hard-on. When he walked up to us, he had a big cock tent standing out in the front. He does not wear briefs, he wears boxer shorts, and what I saw that day definitely told me that Todd was well hung. Damn well hung! Damn that thing was stretching his uniform pants! I have never seen a dick, through a pair of pants, where the head of the dick was as pronounced looking as his was that day! He's got a big head on his dick! And of course as he talked to us, he stood there and rubbed it. Shit man, that made me that much hornier! The longer he rubbed it or touched it, the bigger and bigger it got! I had wanted to play with him for as long as I had known him, which was probably about three years, and seeing that cock outline, and that head outline, that he was showing that day, really made me go wild for him! I had never seen a dick so outlined in a pair of pants like his was then!"

"Todd is 34 now, he stands about six foot two or three, has a baseball player's build. You know what I mean? Real strong muscular legs and a strong muscular butt that fills out every inch of whatever pants he puts on. He's got a good upper body too, goes well with his butt, but his build below the waist line is as hot as a hot rod on the road! I love it! I have always thought baseball players have hot looking butts and legs because of all of the running they do. Shit man, when I watch one of the pro teams, all I see, is what is below the belt!"

"Oh, anyway! Todd kind of snuck up on us. He had been real quiet and of course we weren't expecting anybody out there, that far out at that time of day, so we never knew he was there. When he came over to where we were, I was leaning over an old stone wall that used to have plants behind it, and Sam was ramming my ass with all his might! I definitely was way beyond listening for somebody to be walking up on us. I had a ragging hard-on that I was rubbing up against the stone wall as Sam was ramming my ass, and he and I were just about ready to cum, at the same time, when Todd came up and said something. You know to this day, I still can not remember just exactly what he said. All I know was it was something that ended up sounding real sexy to me, and instead of me getting all flustered that somebody else was there, whatever in the hell he said, made me shoot like some damn horse. I wish I could remember how he let us know he had been watching! I wish I could remember what in the hell he said! All I can remember is it hit Sam and me both right where it felt the best, and that was in the dick. I shot like a damn cannon, and I felt Sam load my ass with what I thought was a fire hose. Shit man! I remember that! I think that was the hottest, me cumin, and me getting loaded, all at the same time that I have ever had!"

"Well what did that Todd guy say then? I mean I know you can't remember exactly what he said, but I mean, —you said he was rubbing his dick. What happened?" Bill inquired of his new friend that was now spouting one ragging, un-clothed, hard-on, as he related his forest fucking session.

"I can remember that I turned as far as I could to see who was talking, and at the same time shooting my cum all over the wall, and of course almost wilting since I saw it was Todd, and I had actually been praying that something like this would happen, so that maybe I might, —I prayed, —maybe I might, —get a chance to play with Todd. Todd was standing there rubbing that great big bulge that was sticking out in the front of his pants, and was also starting to show a wet spot right at the end of his baseball bat sized dick. Well, —you know, it really was not that big, but shit man, looking at it sticking out like it was, it almost did look that big, right then. You guys made comments about mine a minute ago, —well let me tell you, —mine is a fucking midget compared to his! Shit man, he has got one big rod!"

"Sam just stood there with his dick up in my ass, and hell, —I don't know what I did! I think I just wilted to the ground. I do remember I took one hell of a deep breath. Todd then said something like, 'Damn man. Is his ass that good? Sam, you sure are using his ass like it's something good. I've never fucked some guy's ass before, but watching you go for it, it must feel good. Maybe I should finally find out what fucking some guy's pearly little white ass is like. Should I fuck you Brian? Want me to see if I like your butt hole as much as Sam does?'"

"Right then I thought I was going to fucking faint on the spot. My prayers had been answered! I could not believe what I was hearing! I almost yell, 'Hell Yes,' back to him! I wanted his dick so damn bad right then. I had wanted him and me to play for a long time, but I never thought I'd get to, let alone have him suddenly appear and within about 90 seconds ask me if he can fuck me! I had never seen him have a hard-on before, and I really did not know he was hung that damn long. I had figured, or at least had hoped that he was really well hung, but I'd never had anyway to find out before! I stood there in shock! He had just asked me if he should fuck me! I thought, I had died and gone to heaven!"

"Sam pulled his dick out of my butt and I turned to see Todd dropping his uniform pants down to his ankles, and I got my first actual look at his man rod that actually was so long and so hard, that it had pushed his shorts up out of the way so that it could escape out and stand at full attention. The end of his cock was wet with pre-cum. My ass was already wet with Sam's spit and of course his sperm juices that he had just deposited up in there, and so Todd did not need any more lube on his rod. I guess, —or I was just so damn excited that I was finally getting his cock up in me, that I never felt any pain if his rod was too big for my ass hole. I was so damn excited that I was finally getting fucked by this hunk, that he could have fisted me and told me it was his dick, and I would have managed to get my ass open far enough for it! Seriously guys, I was so damn excited about what was happening, that if he had rammed something other than his dick up in me, I would have let him. My life was in his hands, and I was a complete and total, submission to him. I had dreamed of this happening to me, for way too many nights trying to go to sleep, for me to even think of saying I can not take it! I had jerked myself off so many nights trying to make believe that he and I were having sex together, that really, I was having trouble realizing that he was actually fucking my ass."

"He moved up behind me, said, bend over boy, took ahold of that damn rod of his and made hay! I really don't know if he knew right then or not that a man's ass hole is actually only so big or not, but he went up in me like he had never fucked anything before in his entire life. He acted like this was something that he had always wanted his entire life, and this was the first time he had ever gotten it. He slammed me up against that stone wall to where my stomach actually got some black and blue marks on it. Not once did I tell him to slow down or stop or anything. I was finally getting what I had been praying for, and I was in heaven!"

"I really did not know it until later that night, when Sam told me, but while Todd was fucking me like some damn steam locomotive, Sam had gotten back behind Todd and tongue fucked him as much as he could, since Todd's ass was in a very active movement mode. Sam told me that he got up in Todd's butt cheeks far enough to get his tongue up into Todd's ass hole a couple of times and actually got it to open up once. Sam told me he, as he put it, made love to Todd's ass. He sucked on it, he chewed on it, he licked on it, and he tried to wear it on the tip of his nose. He told me that of all of the admiring that I had done over how good Todd's ass looked, I was completely right. He said that he was not jealous at all that I was the one getting the ass fucking, because he thought maybe Todd's ass was the hottest part of him. Of course, a couple of weeks later when the three of us were out, all together again, —then Sam did find out just how great that telephone pole does feel, up inside of you!"

"Todd was pounding my ass as strongly as he could, and I could tell he was getting really hot and getting about ready to shoot a load. And the way he was using my ass, I knew that when he shot, it was going to be one hell of a big load! Of course, like I said, I did not know, that at that same time, that Sam had his face rammed up in Todd's butt. I'm sure that was damn hot for Todd, since that was the first time that he had ever felt some guy's face pushing on his ass hole."

"Todd had grabbed around my chest and was hugging me like a fucking bear! I was breathing real heavy anyway, and with his arms around me as tight as they were, I had real trouble getting air. All of a sudden in my ear I heard him yell, —I'm cummmin!!!! Oh man! Oh shit!! Oh man! I'm cummmmmmin!!!! Oh shit man, —I'm cummmin!!!!"

"I kid you not, I think he dumped at least a pint of thick black man cum juice right up in my butt that night! It hit the inside of me like a fire-hose that got turned on all of the way, all at once, all of a sudden! After he shot me up, he kept pumping me like he had not even cum yet. He grabbed me, he hugged me, he started telling me, 'I'm fucking your cute little white ass man, I'm fucking you,' and he kept that up for probably another four of five minutes, before he even acted like he had shot his wad. Shit man! My ass was so damn sore! I'm not lying men, I thought maybe I had been fucked with one of the old tree logs that had been laying around out there. I really had never been with a guy before that fucked me harder after he shot off, than he did before he shot off! Shit man, what a fucking!! I got it good that day! I thought Sam was feeling good up in my ass, but hell, I wish I could start to explain what in the hell it was like, to get fucked by Todd and his damn big enormous rod!"

"All I can really remember about us getting done together, was that he kept yelling something in my ear about how damn nice, hard and tight my ass was on his dick. Every time he said that, he rammed it back up in me again. Of course I never told him to stop, —for fear that he would never do it again, but shit man, —my ass was getting damn sore! After he finally pulled out of it, I dripped cum out of my ass for at least ten minutes. I mean it just kept coming out. I tried to shit some of it out, and I guess I did, but then when I stood up again, it continued to drip."

"After he pulled his fucking telephone pole, dick out, I kind of turned and looked at it. I knew I needed to take one long look at it so that I could always remember just what in the hell had been rammed up in my ass that night! That was the first real chance I had, to really see what had been rammed up in me! I was afraid that I'd never get it again, and at the same time wondered if I'd ever be able to heal up, back there, enough to take it again. Shit man, the pain that you get from getting something that damn big up in your ass is really weird. Your ass hurts, but for some weird, funny reason, you like it, you love it, and you are glad that you got it! All I can say now about that is, —thank God, Todd likes it as much as I do! He's got more seniority than I do, so he gets to do the scheduling and assignments most of the time, so he sets things up so that he and I, and sometimes Sam too, go out on the overnighters. Damn I come back whipped and tired the next day! He uses my ass almost the entire night when we are out together.

Really, —I come back sleepy and tired. Seriously, he will fuck me until three or four in the morning, and then we get up at sunrise. I don't know how he can come back acting so damn refreshed. I have to admit, that once in awhile I do kind of hope that he schedules Sam to go along too. When he does, that gives me a little relief while Sam is getting fucked. Sam likes it, I'm sure, but I really don't think maybe he is as excited about that much up in his ass as I am. And I kind of think Todd is aware of that too! He uses my ass more often than he does Sam's. I will say one thing though, —Todd needs to be housed at a dairy farm. He puts out as much milk as the cows do! And honestly, I do think he could be one of the bulls!"

"Oh shit men!" Bill exclaimed. "Damn men! Just picturing you getting it up the ass like that, Brian! That has got me so damn hot and horny! Let's get this car unloaded and get this stuff in the cabin, and then I want to go do some lakeside fucking! We've got just about enough time for us to have a good three way down by the water edge before Tom gets here later, and I intend to do as much outdoor fucking and sucking as I can get done. So I think we need to get a move on! We didn't come all the way up here to just stand around and talk about wild sex, —we came up here to do it. Let's move, men!"

"I agree!" Jim replied. "I thought I was kind of horny before, but shit Bill, I agree! For being some guy that 24 hours ago had never messed around with another guy, nor even wanted to, listening to Brian tell us about getting it up in the ass like he did by that Todd guy, has got me so damn worked up, I'm ready to go find some log to use on myself. Bill, you stood there and looked at Brian's cock the whole time he was tell us about Todd and the size of cock he was using. You're anxious to get Brian's big rod pushed up in your ass, aren't you? That big stick of his, kind of turns you on a lot, doesn't it?"

"Hell yes it does, and Jim, don't you even try to act like that cock is not the hottest damn thing that you have ever seen. You are huffing and puffing over that thing as much as I am! We might have both been scared shitless when we found out somebody was up there on the hill top with us, but I kind of have one hell of a big feeling, that as you and I are both standing here looking and drooling over his big cock, that you and I are both damn glad, right now, that he found us up there. And, —I think it's time we start using him and his, —dick of death, —and let him start using our little ass holes. Come on guys, I need to get fucked!"

"Brian, please, please tell us that you like to fuck, as well as you like to get fucked!" Jim pleaded.

"I'm usually Todd's bottom boy, so hell yes guys, I love to fuck! And since I'm usually on the bottom any more, I will really enjoy being a top guy for a change! My dick is ready, and it kind of sounds like you guys are ready to try it. Come on men, let's go fuck! I wanna fuck some ass!"

CHAPTER TEN:

On The Dock

"It is now after two o'clock and I am hungry as hell!" Jim announced as he and his two naked companions went into the house. "I'm gonna fix me a sandwich to eat before we head down to the lake. Do you guys want something to eat?"

Brian and Bill agreed that yes, they could use something to eat too, and offered to help Jim fix some sandwiches but accepted his refusal when he turned and said, "Hey guys. I think it might just be better if I fixed the sandwiches myself, since it kind of looks like the two of you are a hell of a lot more interested in hot dogs, than ham and cheese sandwiches."

Brian and Bill had found themselves rather involved in each other's physical attributes, and Jim had noticed that they were man-handling each other's equipment, and experiencing the joys of having some good long man cock in each of their hands.

"Jim," Bill said. "Jim, have you got a ruler or some kind of a measuring tape around here. I want to see just how big this damn dick of Brian's is. I have to admit that I thought maybe I had a pretty good sized dick, but shit man, look at this damn thing!"

Jim told Bill where he would find a ruler, and after retrieving it, Bill knelt down in front of Brian and took ahold of his dick.

Brian looked down at Bill and said, "Hey Bill. If you want it to get good and stiff before you measure it, reach up here and squeeze my tits some. My cock and my tits are definitely connected together, and if you pinch 'em some, it will really make my dick good and strong."

Bill took Brian's suggestion and while letting his mouth move up nice and close to Brian's already enlarging rod, he reached up with each hand and took ahold of each tit.

"Yeah, Bill! Yeah, pinch my tits man! Yeah, I love that! Oh yeah Bill, that feels so good!"

Jim turned to see what was happening, —to witness Bill using his face up against Brian's cock and crotch, and pinching Brian's tits, as Brian had asked him to do.

Jim grinned and told his buddy, "Hey Bill, suck on that dick! Let me watch you put his dick in your mouth. Mine is the only one you have ever had in there, and now I want to watch you chew on his. Come on man, —chew on Brian's big, thick, dick!"

Bill took a deep breath, looked over at Jim, then looked up at Brian, and then, very cautiously and carefully, he put Brian's dick in his mouth. He pinched Brian's tits as he slowly moved his mouth back onto the rod as far as he could.

"Yeah man! Yeah!" Jim almost yelled. "Yeah Bill, that is hot! You have that damn big dick of his down in your throat! Chew on it, Bill! Chew on it! Suck on it man! Suck!"

Bill continued playing with Brian's tits and chewing and sucking on his cock, and Jim went back to fixing the three, some sandwiches.

Soon Jim announced, "Hey guys! You have some sandwiches and some beer ready, whenever you guys can break loose and so desire!"

Bill pulled off of Brian's dick, and grabbed the ruler. Placing it on the top of Brian's steel stiff dick, Bill almost yelled out, "Oh shit Jim! This damn thing is nine and about a quarter or a half inch long! Oh my God Jim, come here and look!"

Jim came over to where Bill was doing the ole, — measuring the dick thing, and he agreed, 'Yeah, you are right! It sure is! That is one damn hot stick man! Hey Bill, let me wrap this string around it so we can take if off and measure how damn big around it is."

Bill held the end of Brian's dick, to hold it steady, and Jim wrapped a string around it, that he had found in a kitchen drawer. After wrapping the string around and marking where the end connected, he removed it, straightened it out on the ruler and exclaimed, "Oh shit man! Bill that damn fucking cock measures right at seven and a half inches around! Shit man, no wonder that damn thing looks so big! Hell it is big! And you actually had that thing in your mouth!"

"Yeah, I did, and just as soon as we eat, I want that damn thing in my ass, —if we can get it in there! I am really anxious to see if I can take it!"

"Yeah, you'll be able to take it!" Brian assured him. "I've never had any guy yet that can't take it. Your ole ass hole will open up for it! It might look too big right now, but when it starts up in your ole ass hole, it will fit! When we do it, I'll take it nice and slow so that you can feel all of it going up in you, OK?"

"Well all I can say right now is, —when you put that thing up in my butt you had better go good and slow! I want some ass left after you get it back out!"

Brian looked at Jim and Bill both, and said, "Men, believe me, if I can take Todd's big thick, black, pole of a dick, up in my ass, a man's ass will open up just like it's about ready to give birth to a baby. Believe me, cause that's just about what his feels like up in there!

After Bill and Jim did stand there for a few more moments and admired the "dick of death' that they had managed to include into their cabin week-end visit, the three naked, and hard-on men, managed to eat the sandwiches and drink the beers that Jim had fixed for them.

"OK guys. You two guys know this area. You're pretty sure there isn't anybody around here that might find us if we go out there by the lake and do some fucking, right?" Bill asked of his two hunky, horny, naked, and ready friends.

"No Bill. I'm pretty sure we are pretty well back here all by ourselves. Nobody bothers to use that old road when they don't have to, and hardly anybody knows this lake is even back here. Just about the only other ones that even know about it are the rangers, and Brian would know if anybody was back here for any reason, right Brian?" Jim said and asked of Brian.

"Yeah, I'm the one that is supposed to be back here checking stuff out. All the rest of the guys are on the construction job this week-end, and I'm the only one not up there, so I'm pretty sure we are all alone. Now, —Tom does know how to find us right, guys?"

"Yeah, I gave him very expressive instructions before we left the roadside rest area. He acted like he pretty well knew this area. He knew what roads I was talking about." Jim replied.

"OK guys!" Bill intercepted. "Somebody is stalling in getting down to the lake area, and I am getting more and more anxious as I look at that pole on Brian, so let's us get our asses going! My ass is hungry, and it wants a big hot dog! Come on guys, let's go do some lake side fucking!"

As the men walked down the path toward the lake, Bill saw a boat dock that he had not been aware of before. "He guys! I want to stretch out on that dock while I get my ass fucked! OK? Can we fuck there?"

"Sure if you want to." Jim answered.

"I don't care where we do it, I just know that I had better find someplace pretty damn soon since I am about ready to drop one of you two right here and load some ass." Brian stated. "You guys are taking the lead, and I am back here watching those two bare asses walking up in front of me, and I have got to tell you that every time either one of you guys take a step forward and your ass swings to the side, it makes my dick that much harder. So guys, just get me someplace pretty quickly or I am going to tackle some ass from right where I am!"

Bill turned and looked at Jim, and Jim returned the look. They both then turned and looked back at Brian. Bill then said, "Shit man. I'm surprised that you don't fall forward with that much stiff meat flopping around out in front of you man! How in the hell do you keep your balance?"

Brian laughed and replied. "I guess maybe that's why I always want to lay down when it gets hard. Not that I'm ever anxious to stuff it up inside of someone's ass, I guess I just loose my balance!"

As Bill continued to look back at Brian and his dick, Bill said. "Shit man! I don't know if I'm going to be able to take that damn big thing up in my ass or not. The more I look at it, the more I wonder if I can really get that much meat up in me."

"Hey Bill." Brian said to Bill as he placed his hand on Bill's shoulder. "There have been a lot of guys before you that said the same damn thing, and Bill there is not a one of them that did not take it. And most of them said later that they had wished that there was more. Don't worry man, you will take it. We will just take it slow and let you take a little at a time. If I can take Todd's dick, then I know damn well that any guy can take mine. You'll take it man, and you will love it!"

The three men went on, to the dock, and Bill spread down a blanket that he had brought from the cabin. He immediately laid down on it, on his gut, and told Jim to sit down right by his face and get his cock ready for some sucking.

"Jim my man, I want your dick in my mouth while Brian tries to put that fucking big dick of his in my ass! Before today, I had never thought that I'd want a dick in my mouth and a dick up in my ass before, but shit man, last night and today's activities, sure as the hell, have changed me! I am real, —real fucking hungry for that damn big dick to be put up in my ass, and to get your big rod pushed down my throat! I want to be used by you two guys! I guess I just want to be a gay whore boy! Fuck both ends of me at the same time guys! Let me know what really getting used by two guys at the same time is really like! Jim fuck my face! Brian, fuck my ass! Make me some kind of a gay slut, guys. Use both ends of me guys!"

Without further comments, all three men assumed their rather required positions. Bill was on his stomach with his ass twitching for some dick, Jim sat down with his crotch right at Bill's chin, and Brian was smiling and breathing heavy as he lowered himself down onto Bill's butt.

Brian had placed one foot on the outside of Bills torso, and with his left hand, pointed the tip of his rod right at Bill's ass hole. He bent over and dropped a mouth full of spit onto his dick and rubbed it on his cock with the pre-cum that was already there. Then he repeated the same action with the spit falling directly onto Bill's ass opening spot. He rubbed Bill's ass so that his spit would work itself nicely into Bill's hungry and anxious rose spot. Bill twitched and moved as he felt his ass being rubbed by Brian's fingers.

Brian balanced himself and slowly squatted down so that his enormous dick could start it's entry into Bill's ass. Being balanced on his feet and not on his knees, Brian was able to bounce up and down as he allowed his steel rod to enter and then retreat from just the tip of Bill's butt hole. Each time that he slightly stood up, and allowed the dick to remove itself from feeling Bill's ass skin, Bill would let out a small moan of disappointment that Brian was not yet pushing his big cock on into his ass.

Bill pulled his mouth off of Jim' cock, slightly turned his head toward Brian and actually cried asking for him to "Please fuck me, Brian! Please Brian! I am so anxious to feel you up in me. Please push it up in me! Please Brian, I need your dick up inside of me! Brian, please stab my ass with you dick! Please man! Please put it in me!"

Brian simply replied, softly, "OK man! OK."

And with that comment, Brian slightly stood up one more time, then came down fully and allowed his enormous dick to slam into Bill's ass as far as it could, and would, go!

Bill screamed, "Oh God, —Oh my God! Ouch! Oh shit man! —Ouch! Oh shit, man! Oh God Brian, —how much did you put up in me? Oh God man! Oh man! Oh shit that hurts!! Oh God Brian, —is the whole damn thing up in me?"

"Hell no!" Brian answered. "Bill, you wanted me too fuck your ass and you begged for it so I assumed you were really ready for it! I gave you as much as I could get to go up in you, but it's only about half way in. You've only got about half of it so far. I've got another four or five inches to go man. You OK? Bill, I really did not intend to hurt you, but,—I do have to admit that when you turned and kind of cried, begging for me to ram you, that really got me all hot and kind of made me turn wild in your ass! I've never had a guy beg for it like you just did, and Bill, I'm sorry if I hurt your ass, but that begging really turned my wild side on! Bill I'm sorry, I shouldn't have rammed you like that! I know I shouldn't have!"

"I'm OK, —I think, Brian." Bill attempted to reply. "Brian, just don't move for a little bit. Brian let me just lay here and see if I can relax my ass some. Oh shit man, my ass is so full! Oh Brian, don't move, lay still for a minute."

Brian repositioned himself so that he held his dick still so that Bill could attempt to get his ass to accept it without more pain. Brian managed to lay down on Bill's back and got off of his feet. He rubbed Bill's back and the back of his neck. Bill had laid his head down and attempted to just relax his entire body. Jim scooted up closer to Bill's head and just kind of squeezed the sides of his head with the insides of his upper legs.

Bill slowly raised his head up a little, and slowly took the tip of Jim's cock back into his mouth. He then pulled off of it and sucked both of Jim's balls into his mouth. He rolled them around in his mouth for a few minutes and he then turned back toward Brian as far as he could and told him, "Brian, start pushing back into me. I think I'm ready now to try and take more of it. Just go slow man!"

Brian did as requested and he slowly pushed his body forward so that more of his big rod would find its way up into Bill's ass. He watched Bill's actions closely to see how Bill was reacting. Bill was reacting good! He chewed and sucked on Jim's cock, which was placed directly right at his face, and he continued to moan back toward Brian, "Go man. Yeah push!"

Brian grabbed ahold of Bill around the chest and pushed his cock in farther. Once again he listened to see if Bill was making any negative sounds. He was not. Brian pushed in farther. He listened. No negative sounds, just a low and acceptable moan of acceptance from Bill. Brian pushed in more. Bill uttered, "Yeah, fuck me. Yeah fuck my ass man! It's OK now. My ass is OK now."

Brian accepted that as meaning that Bill and his ass had finally accepted the size of dick that he was putting into Bill's ass, and Bill was ready for the rest of it. Brian then pushed the cock in as far as he could. The entire length went into its resting place. Brian pushed onto Bill's body and told him, "You've got it man! It is all up in your ass now man! How do you like it man? Feel good to you up in there?"

Bill pulled off of Jim's dick and after rather laying his head down and resting on Jim's left leg, he told Brian, "Yeah man! Yeah, I know I have it! I can tell it's all up in me now. Man, it feels like I've got a whole flag pole up in me. Brian, just kind of jerk it in and out of me a little so I can feel the tip of it up in me. Yeah man! Yeah, I have all of you up in me. Damn man, I like this. I guess I like getting a big fucking."

Bill grabbed ahold of Jim's body, hugged it and said, "Jim I think your buddy is a real gay. Jim, I think a guy has to be a real gay to love this as much as I am right now. Brian's in my ass, and I've got your dick in my mouth, and no straight guy is ever going to say he likes that, but Jim, I do! Jim fuck my face and tell Brian to fuck my ass. Both of you guys fuck me. Fuck the horny guy! Give it to me! Fuck me men! Use me for nasty, nasty fun guys! Use me like some nasty hungry pig gets used!"

Brian heard what Bill had told Jim, and he reacted. Jim reacted too. Jim fucked the mouth, and Brian fucked the ass! Jim fed his dick to his buddy as he looked at him and did ponder, "I wonder if he really is a true gay? He really is excited about getting a dick on both ends at the same time. He's really wanting both ends of his body used. I'm not sure if I can do that or not!"

Brian fucked Bill's ass with more and more force and continued to hear good comments coming from Bill. Brian warned Bill that he was starting to get close to letting a load fly, and he asked Bill if he wanted it up the ass or across his back. Bill simply said, "In my ass! In my ass man!"

Brian increased his motions and his vigor of fucking this almost virgin ass. Bill's begging for being used so roughly and nasty, was really turning him on. He knew that he was going to be dumping an extra big, hot load, and even that made him that much more excited and anxious to load Bill's ass! He thought, "He wants to be used, and I'm doing the best I can to really use him and use his ass!"

"Bill, I'm cummmmmmmin man! You are getting it man! I'm cummmmmmmmin man!" Brian yelled as he pushed his dick in as far as he could and grabbed ahold of Bill as if Bill would attempt to get up and run. "I'm knocking you up man! I'm loading you man! I'm giving you all of my cum man! I'm owning your ass hole right now Bill! You're my slut right now man! You've got your ass full of me, and I'm using you and your ass! I cummin in you man! Take my cum! Take my cum man! Take my cum!"

Bill just yelled back, "Yeah, yeah, —yeah! Knock me up man! I'll have your kid! Yeah man, knock me up!"

As Bill was yelling back to Brian, he was enjoying the feel of Jim's legs kind of wrapped around his face, and as soon as he got done yelling back to Brian, he started kissing the inside of Jim's upper legs and by pushing his tongue out as far as possible, licked and then chewed on the inside of Jim's upper legs.

As Brian collapsed onto Bill's back, after sharing all of his cum with Bill's insides, Bill also relaxed onto Jim's crotch. All three men were in a position to completely enjoy each other. Brian and Jim were kissing over Bill's head and rubbing each other in all places where they could reach. Slowly Brian started to pull his dick out of its warm and tight spot. Slowly he pulled out. Bill pleaded with him to pull it out slowly. "I want to feel it in me, as lonnnnng as possible!"

Finally Brian's long stick was completely out. Bill said, "Oh man! Oh man! Oh Brian that felt so damn good! Oh Brian, thanks for fucking me! Oh Jim, you have got to get him up in your ass! Jim, you have got to feel that too! Jim, let Brian fuck you!"

"Oh, I don't know!" Jim replied. "Bill I saw the pain you had when he stuck that damn big thing up in you. I'm not so sure I need that. Got to admit it sure looks hot though! I'm just not sure I want my ass hurting like that though."

"Hey Jim, don't let what happened to Bill stop you if you want to try it. He got me all excited and kind of made me loose control when he kind of cried for me to put it up in him. I really should have been slower than I was. If you want to try it, I promise this time I will go very slow and really listen to you. I didn't get his ass opened up before I poke it in! I should have done that! I screwed up, I did! If you decide it's just too much, then we'll stop! Want to try it? I'd really like to fuck you at least just a little. You said earlier that you were getting really horny just by looking at it! Come on man. Lay down here and let Bill give you some hugging while I work it up in you. OK?

"Oh shit man!" Jim replied. "I hope like hell I don't regret this, but yes, you are right. Just looking at that thing is making me horny and I'm afraid that if I don't at least try to take it, then I might regret that decision for a long time."

Then looking at Bill, Jim continued. "Hey guy. Will you lay down and kind of let me lay on top of you so you can hug me tight when I start feeling that thing go up in me?"

"Yeah-hell yes Jim. Come here man. Lay down on top of me."

Bill laid down, and Jim then laid down on top of him. With Brian mounting on top of Jim, it was a three stack.

Brian told the men. "Hell, I hope I can get another good hard-on since I just did Bill." Brian straddled Jim's butt, gave himself another shot of spit and gave Jim's ass a good deposit as he had done to Bill's ass earlier. He reached down and started rubbing Jim's back. "Lay still guy. I'm going to put the tip of my dick up at your ass hole. I'll start pushing it in real slow. If I need to stop, you let me know. OK?"

"Yeah, OK!" Jim replied.

Jim grabbed ahold of Bill and told him. "Oh shit man! I'm not so sure of this. I think I am out of my mind for letting him put that damn thing up in my butt. Shit man, I hope this all works out OK!"

"It will Jim. I begged him too fast to slam it in me and he's taking it real slow this time in your butt, so I know you will be OK. Believe me when he gets that whole thing up in there, you are going to be damn glad you let him fuck you. Jim, grab me and when he pushes, you just grab ahold of me and let him push it in. You'll be glad!"

Brian could hear the two men under him talking, and he knew that he needed to take it slow and careful so that Jim did not decide that he could not take it. He slowly pushed and he felt himself enter Jim's ass hole. He immediately stopped. "You OK Jim?" He asked.

"Yeah, I'm OK. I sure did feel that, but I'm OK. You went in didn't you?"

"Yeah I did. I've only got the head in right now, but now, we've got your sphincter open and now it's just pushing on up into you. Hug Bill. You are past the possible pain time now. When I hurt your ass Bill, it was when I pushed in at first wasn't it? It was when I forced your ass open, wasn't it?"

"Yeah, Brian that's when it hurt. Once you got my hole opened up, then if felt good from that time on. Jim, he's in you now, now it's all fun time. Relax and let him feed you some big long dick. Your ass is going to feel fuller than when I fucked you. He's got a lot more dick to give you than I have, so enjoy it. We found ourselves a good, damn good, playmate to have fun with. When he gets done fucking you, you are going to be wishing he was back up in there again. Jim, I think you and I should have been doing this ass fucking a long time ago. Thank goodness last night happened like it did and we finally found out what we had been missing! Getting your ass fucked feels good, doesn't it?"

"Yeah Bill, it does. Brian, push in farther. I'm OK and now that you are in, I'm not afraid anymore. Push in and if you go too far or too fast I'll let you know. OK?"

"Yeah, OK here Jim. Let me know if I need to stop, but for now, I am going to go the whole way."

And he did! Brian grabbed ahold of the two men laying under him, and he thrust his torso so that he was running the entire length of his dick up into Jim's ass.

"Yeah man! Yeah, —fuck me Brian! Brian, push it in hard! Brian, do me! Fuck my butt man! It's feeling good now. Oh shit Bill, thank you for insisting that I get fucked by him. Oh shit man, he is feeling good! Brian, push on my butt hard! Ram that whole damn thing up in me. Fuck me, —oh yeah, —fuck me!"

Suddenly Jim thought to himself, "Oh shit man! I think I know now why Bill was begging to be played with like a slut. Shit man, I think I understand. This is hot! Shit man, this is good!"

Brian was rather surprised at how well this was going for himself, since it had only been a few minutes since he had completely dumped his entire cum load up into Bill's ass, and at that time, he thought he was completely out of energy. He had regained his energy and he was giving Jim as much active ass fucking action as he had given to Bill's ass.

From his position on the bottom of the stack, Bill could tell that both of the men lying on top of him were in a "good place". He had Jim grabbing him and hugging him and moaning with great pleasure each time that Brian pumped his ass. Brian was expressing the same pleasures as he humped and bumped Jim's hungry ass. Bill was enjoying the idea that two guys were having man to man sex on top of himself. He realized that he was acting as the mattress for two very horny guys that were truly enjoying each other. One enjoying an ass to fuck, and the other one enjoying having his ass fucked. Bill realized that his position was rather unusual. But, he did not have any complaints about getting to be the man that had two hungry and active fuckers, going to each other, over the top of him, and using him as the cushion under them.

Suddenly Brian loudly screamed out, "I'm cummmmmin man! Jim,—Bill, I'm cummmmmin! — Oh shit man! I did not know if I would be able to so soon. Oh men, —I'm cummmmin!"

"Oh Bill, he feels so good in me. Oh God, his cum is hot inside! Oh Bill, —was his juice hot when he fucked you? Oh man it feels hot up in there. Oh Brian, push on my ass! Yeah, —pussssssssssh! Yeah man! Oh Bill, I just got fucked!! Oh shit man, I just really got fucked! I got fucked big time!"

Bill grabbed Jim and gave him a hug. Brian completely collapsed on top of Jim. "Oh shit man! Now I am exhausted! Oh man, that felt so good! Jim, —you and your ass, OK?"

"Yeah Brian, yeah it sure is man! Thank you so much! I am so glad you and Bill both insisted that I get fucked by you. I am really, really glad! Your dick feels really good up in there!"

After a few minutes of resting, all three men finally unloaded their stack and rolled onto their separate spaces.

"Hey guys!" Bill said. "Is that water warm enough to swim in, or is it cold?"

"No, it's pretty warm!" Brian replied. "Let's all jump in and kind of wash ourselves up some. Want to guys?"

"Yeah," both men responded.

Suddenly, all three men dove into the cool lake water.

After a short time in the water, Jim told the other two that he felt they needed to get back toward the cabin just in case Tom happened to show up earlier than he had figured he could. "I don't what him wondering if he's in the wrong place if he gets here and can't find us."

The three gathered up the blanket, the only thing they had carried to the dock, and headed back up the path toward the cabin.

"So Brian. I assume Tom will recognize you when he sees you, right?"

"Yeah, Jim —I guess he will. I'm sure he has seen me in the bars before, but I'm sure he won't know what my name is. I doubt that he knows who I am. I know one thing, I sure am going to be happy that I finally get a chance to meet him. I hope like hell he does not object to having some sex fun with me. I've wanted to play with that body of his ever since I first saw him! He likes to tongue fuck, right guys? Shit man! I hope he likes to dick fuck too. I want him up in my ass! And I will tell you one more thing, —I sure will be willing to do some of his 'Tom Tongue' things to his ass, too! I'd love to have my face pushed up in that ass. Hey guys! When Tom gets here, I kind of think we need to get ourselves in a daisy chain, and all of us lick and tongue an ass in front of each of us. Yeah, —four guys on their hands and knees, in a circle, licking and tonguing each other's asses! Yeah man! Yeah, I'm ready for that!"

CHAPTER ELEVEN:

The Four Way

Jim, Bill and Brian returned back to the cabin and enjoyed some good general conversation finding out about each other, and in Bill and Jim's case, finding out a lot about Brian's life in the gay community. Neither man had been too interested about how "the other half" lives, but they now found out that perhaps they had been avoiding a subject that perhaps they should know a little more about. The "two straight guys" did each admit that they felt that, from this time on, they were going to be feeling a little different about some men that they personally worked with that they knew were gay.

Being a store manager, Jim did agree that he probably had more gay guys working for him than he had ever thought possible, and Bill had to admit that now, he had a new and different outlook on life, and some of the possibilities in life. He was going to be a little more aware of some of the things some of his co-workers did and talked about. He mentioned a couple of guys, that he now has a little more than just a passing interest in knowing, a little more, about. Such as, how they spend their private time, more than he did before. "Shit men. I've never looked at those two guys with any real interest, but I'm not so sure now that I will not be noticing them and their actions a lot more closely. Now that I think back about it, there are a couple of times that some of their comments could have been kind of a come on, or at least an attempt to see how I reacted, and now I am going to be listening to those comments a lot closer. Especially if it comes from that guy they call Copper. He wanted to become a cop when he was younger, and so he gained the nickname Copper. It sure wasn't the body build that stopped him from being a cop. He wears just T-shirts and cut-off Levis as often as he can, and damn man, I don't blame him. If I looked like he does, that's all I'd wear if I could get away with it. And you know, I think he is one of those guys that if he was maybe going over the edge of what was normally allowed, he could get away with it simply because nobody would want him to change and act more conservative, or look more conservative. When you look that damn good, people let you get away with stuff others don't get to. You know, I never wondered about him. I just kind of figured he was screwing every girl he wanted, but now that I think about him, I wonder! He gets picked up from work by different guys quite often, and although he is always talking about his ball games and stuff with the guys, he never talks about any dates. Hmmm—I wonder!"

As they were kicking back and enjoying the conversation, Tom pulled into the drive area. All three men, still naked as a polar bear, went out to greet him.

"Well, shit men!" Tom exclaimed as he got out of his Jeep. "Shit, I certainly did not expect to have this great of a greeting when I got here."

"Hey, Tom! Welcome man!" Jim expressed.

"Tom, I'm glad you are here. Tom, do you know Brian?" Bill asked.

As Tom checked out Brian and his hanging equipment, he commented, "Well I sure have seen the face around before, but I sure as hell have never seen the rest of him! Shit man, if you guys had told me earlier that this kind of a package was included, I would have gotten somebody to cover for the rest of my day and I would have been up here a lot earlier!"

"Brian," Tom said as he extended out his hand. "I am damn glad to meet you! All of you!" He added as he emphasized that he was checking out Brian's cock.

"How in the hell is it that you and I have been hanging out in some of the same bars and I was never made aware of your, —more impressive parts, man?" Tom asked as he once again cased out the entire package of Brian.

"Well." Brian replied. "I guess all I can say is, you never asked. Tom, I have checked you out for a long time now, and when I was told by Jim and Bill that you were coming up after you got off of work, I will admit I immediately got a hard-on. I've wanted to play with you for a long time, so I sure do hope our being here together works out well for the both of us then!"

"Jim, Bill, —I thought you guys told me earlier that you guys were straight. How in the hell do you two know Brian? Shit! I wish you had told me earlier that he was going to be here too. Of course you would have had to tell me that he hangs a fucking big bratwurst sausage, since I was totally unaware of that! Shit men, have you guys been fucked by him?"

"Come on in Tom." Jim said as he threw his hand up on Tom's shoulder and rather guided him toward the cabin. "We've got a lot of explaining to do to bring you up to speed. We met you first, before we got caught fucking, —by Brian here!"

"Oh shit man!" Tom exclaimed. "I caught you two sucking on each other, and then on the same day, Brian catches you two fucking? Come on man! Really, you have got to fill me in! This is getting way too much to believe! God, you two must have sex everywhere and all of the time, if you got caught twice in the same day. OK,—what happened, I've got to hear this!"

Bill, Jim and Brian filled Tom in on the actions that had happened that day, and how Brian had found them on the hill top, after he heard them screaming about getting fucked and doing the fucking!

Tom's main interest was finding out about the "two straight guys" getting fucked by such a big dick.

"Yeah right! If you two guys each got fucked by that damn big stick of meat, don't either one of you try and convince me again that you are straight guys. Hell, I have known that I am gay for probably 15 or 16 years, and I have never been fucked by something that damn big, and on your very first day of playing around with guys, you both get it up the ass by that? No damn fair! No fair! Shit man, Brian, why in the hell didn't you let me know you were hanging that much? Wait, —hey wait a minute! You know a few months ago there was all of that secret stuff over at the, 'He Gay, I Gay Bar', about some guy that was really, really hung, but the guys that had gotten fucked by him wouldn't tell us who he was. That was you, —wasn't it? You are the big cock guy that they were talking about and the rest of us were trying to figure out who in the hell it was. Shit man! Shit, when they were talking about it one night, I looked at you and asked him if you were the guy and he said, "No". Brian, are you the guy that fucked Jack Omen out in the back of his truck one night? Are you the guy?"

Shaking his head kind of slowly, Brian told Tom that yeah, he was the fucker. They had been in the bar drinking and both of them had gotten pretty tipsy, and when Jack reached over and grabbed Brian in the crotch, Brian had gotten a hard-on, and when Jack felt it, he insisted and demanded that he either get fucked with that dick, or he was going to de-pants Brian right there in the bar.

"We used the bed of his truck since it was out back of the bar, and neither one of us thought we should be driving anyplace. Two guys that were leaving the bar found us, and, so that they would promise to never admit what had happened out there, I had to fuck both of them too. So that's why nobody would say who it was. They had promised to keep their mouths shut. The owner of the bar is still trying to find out just who was involved, and we don't want him to know, so promise that you will not tell anybody, OK?"

"Yeah, OK! Well, yeah OK, —as long as I get the payback that those two guys got to keep their mouths closed. You fuck my ass too, and then I will keep it a secret too. OK?"

"Hell yes!" Brian replied. "I don't need something like that though, to make me fuck your ass! Hell Tom, I have licked my lips over watching you just walk through a bar so many times, that when they told me who they had found and asked to come up and join in, I damn near cum in my pants! Tom, I get to fuck your ass, and as I hear it, —you are quite an ass kisser, right? They tell me you like to do the "Tom Tongue" thing! Anyway, that's what Jim and Bill call it! I'll fuck your ass and you eat out my ass, OK?"

"Oh, hell yes! Oh shit men! This is turning out to be one hell of a lot wilder time than I expected, and just thinking that I was coming up here to play with a couple of good looking guys, —that were just now getting into the gay stuff, that was exciting all by itself! Shit man! This is great!"

"OK, OK guys!" Bill intercepted. Three out of the four of us are standing here letting the whole world know that we have raging hard-ons, and number four is still standing there like he is getting ready to go to church or something. Tom, get rid of the clothes man! You're making me embarrassed. I'm standing here totally nude and you are still all tucked in tight! And beside man! I can see your boner sticking out the front of those pants."

Tom immediately stripped everything off. "There, better? I feel better! Shit man! I still can not believe what is developing here. Two, —what they claim are, —straight guys, —that are just getting started with the fun stuff in life, me the little gay guy that never gets any, and ole Brian over here with the rod off of some stallion horse! Shit man, this is turning out to be a real life porno film!"

"What in the hell do you mean, you, the gay guy that never gets any? Hell Tom, —the only reason you have never found out what I have is because every time I see you in one of the bars, you have so many guys hanging onto you and dreaming about being in bed with you, that I never got a chance to kind of hint that I'd really like to ram my little dickie up in your tight ass hole! Shit man! Whenever you leave the bar, you have at least three guys huffing and puffing out the door with you. Tom, you get it all the time! Shit man, I'm surprised that you could find the time to be up here tonight. Man, you are probably putting four or five guys in a state of depression since you're not at the bar tonight! Don't give me that shit that you never get any! I know one thing man, you sure as the hell are going to tonight, so get your ass ready man!"

"Tom let me tell you!" Bill entered. "When he says get your ass ready, he means it! Yeah, I've got to admit that I've only been fucked by Jim and Brian so far, but I kind of think Jim will agree, that to get Brian's cock rammed up in your ass, it's a little different than just getting fucked! It's more like having the Atchison, Topeka and Santa Fe running up in there. He goes up in there, it's like a whole train up in there!"

"Well, all I can say then, —is, get me a fucking railroad track, because I want to feel that damn big thing up inside of me!"

Jim looked at Bill, rather laughed and remarked, "You know man! This is kind of funny to me. Here we are, the two straight guys, and we got fucked by a dick, like that, before Tom has, and he's been out playing around for 15 or 16 years. I feel pretty proud of what we've done! I guess we've been fucked by one of the best, so they'd say!"

"Well, if not the best, at least the largest!" Bill replied.

"Oh no, guys!" Brian jumped in. "No, no! Probably not the best, and I know damn well not the largest. That title is Todd's! Believe me, I know first hand, or maybe I should phrase that as, —first assed! His cock, in my ass! Now that is big!"

"Todd? Who is Todd?" Tom very quickly and very interestingly asked. "Who in the hell is Todd? If you are saying he is bigger than you, who in the hell is he? Somebody that has fucked you, I guess?"

Brian filled Tom in on the details about Todd, but then of course made Tom promise to keep all the information about Todd a complete secret!"

"Yeah, I'll keep my mouth shut, but maybe I need to do the same kind of a deal as you did with Jack Omen! If you will get him and me together, get him to fuck my ass, then I will make sure I will keep him a total secret. Hell, if for no other reason than to keep him to just ourselves so that he's not out fucking every hungry open ass hole that is in this part of the country!"

Jim offered his guests something to eat, and after getting it ready, all four men sat down at the table and enjoyed a great time together, talking mostly about stuff that Bill and Jim had never discussed, nor even thought about wanting to discuss. They had the opportunity to find out a lot about how gays live, what they normally did when they got together, what type of sex action most guys liked the best, and even some conversation about why some guys do drag. They hit on about every gay and sex subject, in some form or another, that Jim and Bill could think to ask about!

Brian and Tom asked, how did Bill and Jim think they were going to be able to handle their new found sexual fun, since it had to be kept such a total secret. That question received a, —"Well, I'm not sure right now!" from Bill, and a, —"I'm not sure either!" response from Jim.

Jim followed through with, "Well men. I kind of think that after I get home, I am just going to have to accept the fact that this week-end was definitely a different kind of a week-end, but then it is time to get back to reality and back to the normal way of living. I won't deny that if it is possible for Bill and I to sneak off someplace for a little while, and re-do part of this week-end again, sure, I'll take advantage of it! But, for normal living, it's got to be the normal life again."

"Yeah Jim's right. We are married guys and we do live a different kind of a life than this, and so I guess it will just have to be back to normal, —but, —hey, —" as he looked at both Brian and Tom and broke out into a big grin, "before we split this week-end, I want to know how to get in touch with both of you guys for,— just in case I have time and Jim's not available. I need to know I can get in-touch with you two. OK? Can I? I mean, like can I possibly be able to call one of you, to see if you are available? Can I use you guys as back up? I've got to admit it guys, —I think I know me well enough to know that once this week-end is over, I am not going to be able to just easily forget all about it! I am really finding out in a big way that I like gay sex, and I know I am not going to be able to just let it go. I'm going to need to find it as often as possible. Jim, I know what you are probably thinking right now, but man, I know me. I like this! Maybe I should have been doing this kind of stuff a lot sooner. I'm not going to separate or anything like that, but like the guys have said, there are a lot of married guys out there that have gay sex all of the time, and I know right now, I am going to be one of them. I'm finding the hunky strong and muscular male body too damn exciting to just walk away from it. I guess I've been wanting this kind of action to happen for a long time and I've just never been in the right situation to let it happen. Guys, I know I like having man to man sex, and I am not going to try and deny it!"

"Hell yes, I'll give you my number!" Tom said. "I told you earlier today that guys meet there at the roadside rest all of the time for sex, and if it just happens that it is you and me, well, —we will just have to lock the ole restroom door for awhile, won't we?"

"I don't live quite as close to you as Tom does, but I sure will make myself available anytime you need me." Brian said. "You know I do those overnight things once in awhile, and maybe we can work it out to where if you can get away for a night, we can do the ole, —out in the forest thing together. Or if it's just meeting someplace for a quickie, we can do that too! I'll make sure you can get in-touch with me. We can work out plans! Gay guys, the single ones and the married ones, do that all the time you know!"

Suddenly Tom spoke up. "You guys can sit around and talk about sex all night if you want to, but I'm going to get my ass fucked by Brian's big dick! Come on Brian, I've got to feel that damn big thing up in me!"

"Where am I going to fuck you, man?" Brian asked. "You wanna do it here in the living room on the floor?"

"Yeah that's good with me. I really don't care where, but let's get to it. Is it OK Jim, —Bill, if Brian fucks me? Hey, can you two lay down side by side in front of me so I can switch back and forth from one of you to the other one and do some cock sucking while I get rammed?"

"Yeah sounds good to me if we can get in place right." Jim answered. "You game Bill?"

"Hell yes I am! That's why we are up here at the cabin. To do the stuff we can't usually do. Let's see if that will work OK." Bill answered.

All four men headed for the living room of the cabin and found comfortable places to start some active, sexual actions.

Tom hit the floor on his stomach and told Bill and Jim to lay down on their backs up close to his face. Brian juiced up his dick and Tom' ass with some spit and a little bit of lube that Tom had brought with him, and he then positioned himself on top of Tom's butt. "Ready man?" He asked Tom.

"Yeah, I sure am. Brian, I've been fucked enough to know that a dick that damn big is going to hurt going in the first time, so take it easy on my butt hole. OK? Go in slow, and then after you get it up in me, then you can fuck the hell out of me. I want that damn thing up in me, and when it's up there, I want to be able to really feel it!"

Jim and Bill had positioned themselves right up beside Tom's head so that he could lean over to his left and suck on Jim's rod, and then he could turn to his right and suck on Bill's cock. He started on Jim's stick first and while he was sucking on it, he was stroking Bill's cock and Brian was starting his entry up and into Tom's ass.

As Brian rather quickly slid into Tom's hole, Tom jerked and really clamped down on Jim's dick! He let out a strong moan.

"Hurt when it first goes in, don't it?" Bill asked.

Tom rolled his eyes over toward Bill and rather shook his head. Although he had a mouth full of Jim, he uttered, "Damn big!"

Although it had hurt when Brian first pushed Tom's asshole open and his thick rod was rammed up into Tom's ass, Tom recovered quite quickly, and he started humping his ass to indicate to Brian that he was ready for more, and he was wanting it pretty damn fast!

As Brian got into a rhythm on Tom's ass, Tom also got into quite a rhythm on Jim's cock and soon switched over to do Bill's. He managed to accomplish quite a system approach, of sucking on one dick for a few strokes, and then very quickly throwing his head to the other direction and taking the alternate dick down his throat.

Brian was fucking Tom's ass much wilder and rougher than he had been able to do to with Bill or Jim's ass. He knew that Tom's ass was much more used to having dicks rammed up in it, and he did not take any slow actions in finding out just how rough Tom liked to have his ass treated. He found out very quickly that Tom's ass was a very hungry and a very experienced ass. He pounded it and he felt a great amount of excitement, that he was finally in the tight shaped ass that he had been admiring for so long, but had not had any opportunity to approach, until this glorious day. He was in his glory, finally getting to fuck Tom's grand prize ass. As he raised and lowered his cock into and back out of Tom's ass hole, Brian pondered, "Shit man! I wonder who else has had the chance to fuck this ass? I wonder what class of guys I am now a part of. I'm sure this ass has never been fucked by anybody other then the hottest of studs, and tonight I get to fuck it! Damn, I'm in a new group of people now. When I'm in the bar and Tom is there, I'm going to be one of the main guys, now. I've just entered a whole new group of friends. I'm sure Tom will tell them why I got to fuck him. Shit man! If the description includes the size of my dick, I might be able to pick any guy that I want, at that time. Tom might have the hottest ass in the bar, but if there are any bottom boys there, I'm sure after tonight, and after Tom gets a chance to tell them what my dick is like, I'll get to pick any ole bottom boy I want! Shit man, this is good!" And he then, fucked Tom's ass even harder! In his excitement, he "headed for town!"

Tom pulled off of Jim's dick and kind of turning toward Brian, rather yelled, "Fuck me man! Fuck me hard! Give me that damn rod of yours man! Yeah, yeah, —fuck the hell out of me."

Then turning back toward Jim and Bill he said, "Hey guys, someone give me an ass to chew on. I want to tongue fuck one of you guys! Somebody give me an ass!"

Bill immediately sprung up and threw his ass right in front of Tom's face. He spread his legs apart so that he could back up right at his mouth. He then told Jim, "Hey, Jim, get over here in front of me so I can suck you off while I get my ass sucked on."

Jim repositioned himself so that he was laying on his back right under Bill's face. Bill pushed his ass up in the air so that it was right at Tom's face, and he then lowered his own face down so that he could take Jim's cock rod into his mouth.

Brian was fucking Tom's ass like he was some kind of a jack hammer, Tom had his face completely buried into Bill's ass and with each ram he got in the ass, he then transferred that ram into Bill ass with his tongue, and each time Bill's ass got rammed with Tom's tongue, then transferred that motion onto Jim's stiff rod. And with each thrust onto his cock, Jim returned the favor by throwing his torso up toward Bill's face so that he could force as much cock back into Bill's throat as he could possibly manage! All four men were completely involved in doing another guy. The chain of motion started with Brian's force into Tom's ass and then continued down the line from that ass.

Brian was sweating like a dripping faucet. The sweat was running off of his forehead. He kept leaning his head down and wiping his face on Tom's back.

Tom kept giving Brian more and more ass to fuck with every force that Brian offered to him. Tom kept pushing his ass back like he could not tell if he was getting fucked in as far as possible or not. Although he had a mouthful of ass, he kept uttering in a loud way, "More, Brian, more!! Fuck me more!" He was getting one hell of a hot fucking and he was wanting more. He kept begging for, "More!"

Bill's ass was buried across Tom's face as firmly and as completely as he could get it placed. His ass hole quivered open and closed each time Tom's tongue forced its way in even so slightly. As Bill could feel the tip of Tom's tongue, he pushed his face back as quickly as he could so that he could possibly get more tongue up in there, than he had received the prior times. Even with Jim's big rod stuck back into his throat, he kept begging for Tom to "Lick my ass! Lick my ass! Bite my ass hole!" He kept thrusting his ass back toward Tom's face, his mouth and his tongue! "Lick my ass, bit my hole!" He continued to yell!

Jim's position on his back on the floor right under Bill's face gave him the position so that he could grab ahold of Bill's arms and shoulders and pull him forward and onto his cock with all of the force that he wanted, and at the same time use his bare feet to feel Bill's body and even reach back and feel Tom's face going into Bill's ass. He humped and rammed into Bill's mouth. He grabbed ahold of Bill's head and pulled on him each time when Bill begged for Tom to lick his ass or bite his ass. He could tell every time, when Bill moved his face in Bill's ass. The motion carried down to his dick. He felt like he had Bill's mouth and Tom's mouth on his dick at the same time. He felt like he was the real winner in this stack of guys doing each other since he was the one on the bottom and could feel every movement made by any of the other three guys that were kind of on top of him.

Suddenly Jim started yelling, "Brian, fuck his ass! Fuck his ass hard man! Tom chew Bill's butt! Chew his butt out man! Suck on his ass hole! Suck him! Yeah suck his ass dry! Bite my dick Bill! Bite me! Bite my dick Bill! Yeah guys, do me! Yeah, do me, guys!"

Without warning, Brian started actually screaming that, —"I'm cummmmin man! Tom give me your ass man! I'm cummmmmmin man! Tom, I'm going to load you! I'm cummmmmmin!!!!!"

Brian grabbed ahold of Tom and held him solid and tight! He pushed his dick up into Tom's ass just as far as he could force it to go! He held it there as he felt every bit of cum dump out of his body, and into Tom's! "Oh shit man! Oh shit! Tom, I just shot my wad up in your ass. Tom you have got part of me up in your ass! A big part of me up in there man, a big part!"

Once again, Brian lowered his head down to wipe his face on Tom's back, but this time he did not straighten back up. He laid there. He took deep breaths and grabbed ahold of Tom as tightly as he could.

When Brian started yelling that he was cumin, Tom got so excited that he grabbed both sides of Bill's ass cheeks and pulled apart on them so hard that Bill actually squealed in some pain. Tom opened his mouth as widely as he could, and he took into his mouth as much of Bill's butt, and his asshole as he could. He bit!

He had a complete mouth full of ass, and ass skin, and he bit! He bit hard! Bill jumped!

"Ouch!" Bill exclaimed as he felt Tom's teeth enter his ass skin. "Ouch! Oh man!" Bill again exclaimed. Only, this time, the "ouch" changed to a very acceptable and agreeable "Oh," suddenly. Suddenly the pain turned into excitement and total pleasure. "Bite again! Tom, Tom, bite me again!!!" Bill liked the feeling that he was getting! He liked it a lot! He quickly discovered that he truly loved to get his ass and the area around it bitten as roughly as he could get! "Tom, bite me more please!!!!!!"

As Bill was getting his butt bitten, much to his surprise, but also to his complete pleasure, he yelled to Tom to bite him more and he then immediately, rammed his mouth back down onto Jim's stiff rod, and he jammed it down farther this time than he had attempted to before. He did not worry about choking! He gagged and he struggled for air, but he forced his face down onto Jim's rod as far as he could force his face! He knew he was trying to eat all of Jim. He actually had the feeling that if it was possible, he would swallow the entire man and make him an internal part of himself. He wanted all of Jim to be a part of himself. For a minute, he tried to take all of Jim into himself! He wanted them to be, "one". He knew of no other way to so totally take his man, than to try and take all of him down the throat! He wanted to swallow Jim, all of Jim!

As Brian was screaming that he was cummmin, —Bill felt Tom grab ahold of his dick and jerk on it with all of his might! He shot! It only took a moment of feeling Tom jerk on it before it exploded all of it's cum juices. It was during that cum explosion when Bill tried so desperately to eat all of Jim! And it was when Bill forced his mouth down so completely on Jim's rod, that Jim, so completely, uncontrollably, shot Bill's throat full of his thick juice.

Brian had started the line of cumin! When he yelled out that he was cumin, Tom got so turned on, or actually so much more, since he was already in heaven just getting the fucking that he was getting, that his dick shot his cum with four big spurts, without even being touched. That was when he reached up and grabbed onto Bill's dick, and Bill then immediately shot off and in his tension and excitement got his buddy Jim so hot, that Jim loaded Bill's mouth with all of his juices. Each man had shot his wad with no control. All four men had experienced uncontrolled cumin! Brian's load completely filled Tom's tight ass, Tom's cum wads flew onto the floor right beside Bill's feet, Bill's cum shots hit the floor and on Jim's feet and of course Jim's man juices completely filled Bill's mouth.

Brian collapsed onto Tom's body. Tom laid his head down and onto Bill's ass. Bill pulled off of Jim's dick and rather embarrassed, had to spit out some of the cum that he had not been able to swallow and he then laid his head down on the same dick that had just fed him its entire load. Jim was exhausted. He laid his head down, he laid his arms down, and he quietly said, "Oh shit! Oh shit!"

All four men were whipped. Excited, but whipped.

Tom looked down and said, "Uh ho! Kind of looks like we have some cleaning up to do. We've got cum all over this place! And right now I am afraid that if I stand up, we are going to have some more. I feel like my ass is so full of cum, that when I stand up, it is going to flow!"

"Well, I sure as the hell, know where mine went to, don't I Bill?" Jim asked.

"Yeah, —but I think there must have been more than just one dick shooting off in my mouth for as much cum as I tried to swallow." Bill replied. "Where in the hell did you get so much cum from? I thought you already shot off earlier today!"

"Hey man!" Jim responded. When you actually have three guys on top of you, like I did, and all three guys are cumin all at the same time, it's just going to happen. Shit man, I never knew sex could be that damn exciting! But then, I've never had sex with three people all at the same time before, let alone three guys! Shit man, —what a trip! Bill, I kind of understand what you were saying earlier about how you are going to be needing this as often as possible once this week-end is over."

Then addressing toward Brian and Tom, Jim continued. "Men, I'm with Bill. I want to be sure I know how to contact both of you! Man, my idea about wild sex has just been altered. I've got to do this a lot! A lot and often!"

All four rested where they were for a few minutes, and then one by one they attempted to get up.

"Hey Jim, can Brian and I go in and use the shower?" Tom asked. "He sweat all over me so bad, I need to have him wash me up now so that I am nice and clean again."

Jim of course told the guys to use the shower, and that he and Bill would follow them.

"The only problem is, I didn't figure on this many guys here this week-end, so we may have to share towels since I didn't bring any extra." Jim told the group.

"Well, considering what we all just experienced together, I'm not so sure sharing towels is going to be a big problem. I do kind of mean, —if I can let Brian shoot as much up in my ass as he did, I'm sure a little bit of sharing a towel with him is not a problem." Tom stated, and then continued. "But you do know, putting my face up inside of a guy's ass is totally different than sharing a towel with him."

Almost in unison, the other three all said, as they all grinned and laughed! "Yeah, right man!"

Tom and Brian headed for the shower and Bill and Jim attempted to start cleaning up the cabin, from all of the evidence that four guys had just fucked the hell out of each other.

Bill looked at Jim and asked. "What was it that Brian suggested earlier that he wanted to do after Tom got here. He called it a, daisy chain, right? Where we all get on our hands and knees and chew out the ass in front of ourselves. Right? Should we mention that, or let it go?"

"Hey, as long as I can kick back for just a few minutes and re-coup, I'm game for whatever everybody else wants to do, and since the sun is going down, I think it would be fun for all of us to go out to the dock and have some good ole moon light sex, if you want to. What do you think?"

I think that sounds like a great idea! I need to get my ass fucked, and I'm sure you do too, and I think having all four of us out there and sharing asses with each other is a great idea. I want to get fucked by that Tom guy too! I think he is hot! He's got a good body! His dick might not be as long as Brian's, but I bet he really knows how to fuck an ass!"

"Well, I know for sure that I am going to find out!" Jim asserted. "My ass is ready for it! If he needs practice, he sure as hell can practice in my ass!"

CHAPTER TWELVE:

Some Private Time

After everybody had a chance to freshen up some, and kind of get rested some, Jim was the one that made a mention that his ass was now getting very lonely and sure did need some attention. All four did agree that since the moon was now just coming up from the horizon, that doing a "group get-together" down on the boat dock might be a fun way to experience the cool evening outdoor breeze, and let that breeze mix with the hot sweat that they each knew would develop, once they all got very active.

Brian and Tom took the lead and headed down the bath toward the boat dock. Jim and Bill followed behind, but not very closely.

Bill turned to Jim and said. "Let's play with them some, and then if it's OK with you, I'd kind of like for just the two of us to come back to the cabin and spend some good private time together, OK?"

Jim turned, looked at Bill, spread a broad smile across his face, reached out and grabbed Bill around the waist and replied, "Yeah, yeah, —I really would love that! That sounds great to me!"

Jim then took Bill's left hand in his right hand, and rather picked up his pace a little. He walked with a little more spring in his step. He held his head a little higher. He hummed happy tunes.

As Jim and Bill got to the dock, Brian was spreading a couple of blankets out for the four men to lay on.

"OK guys!" Tom said. "Who's doing who and what's happening here men?"

"Hell, I have no idea." Replied Jim. "You guys are the ones that are a hell of a lot more familiar with this type of getting together than Bill and I are. So how do you guys normally get started? What do you suggest?" He asked, as he felt rather, "out of place," in attempting to organize an event that he had actually never been involved in before.

"OK if we need a lead person here," Brian chipped in, "I need to get my ass fucked by somebody, or maybe by a couple of you guys, if that will get things started!"

Tom then looked at Bill and Jim and asked, "OK guys. Which one of you wants to do the first fucking? Jim, why don't you get up in Brian's ass, Bill, why don't you do your buddy's ass, and I will more than happily slam my face up into your ass Bill while you fuck Jim. How's that sound to everybody?"

There was an automatic sounding of, "OK" from everybody, and very quickly everybody took his required position. Brian was on the bottom, Jim stuffed his ass very quickly as Brian let out a loud moan. He then very quickly said, "Oh, I'm sorry. I'm OK. I guess I just didn't expect you to go in so fast. Jim, it feels good. Fuck me man!"

Bill stood above Jim's protruding ass and immediately sank his entire rod into his buddy's ass. Suddenly Jim let out a squeal and let out a loud moan.

"I'm OK, I'm OK!" Jim said back to his fucker. "I'm sorry! I guess I was like Brian, I just did not expect you to ram me so fast! I'm OK! You feel good in me Bill, fuck me. Tell you what—since you are on top of me, you help me fuck Brian. Fuck my ass and when you punch me, then I'll pass it on to Brian. Brian, you ready for the two of us up here to force as much of me in you as we can?"

"Shit yes! Hell yes, —I'm ready. I wanna feel both of you guys pushing on my ass! This will be kind of a different way of getting double fucked!"

With Jim now firmly planted in Brian's butt, and likewise, Bill also firmly planted in Jim's butt, Tom positioned himself in his favorite position and by grabbing hold of Bill's butt cheeks, and spreading them apart as far as he could, he stuck his tongue out as far as possible and aimed it for the hole. Contact! Entry! He found what he was anxious for! He pushed his tongue up into Bill's butt as far as he could get it to go. He was tongue fucking Bill's ass. He was in heaven! Well, actually, he was really in Bill's ass, but to him, that was the same as being in heaven!

Suddenly Bill was on the receiving end of Tom's place in heaven, and he was starting to feel like maybe he was in heaven too. He started telling, almost yelling, for Tom to, "Tongue my ass man! Fuck my ass with your tongue man! Eat my ass out with your tongue man! Stick my ass with your tongue! Kiss my ass! Kiss my ass! Bite my butt! Get your teeth up in there and bite the edge of my butt hole Tom! Take my ass! Bite me! Yeah,—Yeah, —bite me!"

Bill had already had Tom's mouth back there in his ass earlier that day, and he knew how active Tom could be if he was turned on. Bill's rather yelling at him was an attempt to get Tom's mouth and tongue as excited as Bill could manage. Bill loved the feel of teeth on the edge of his ass hole. "Bite my ass Tom! Bite my ass!" He yelled out.

Bill's yelling at Tom was getting Jim very excited and with each yell, he pumped Brian's ass that much harder, and in respect that made his ass go up and down faster and more forcefully, forcing Bill to attempt to keep up with his movements.

All four men were totally into this great expression of total sexual freedom, enjoying not only their own totally naked, exposed, rough and manly bodies, out in the cool evening air, but the even more fulfilling enjoyment of feeling and enjoying all of the strong and the soft textures of the other three men. The mixture of the strong, firm, male bodies and the gentle, wooded, lakeside and moon lit environment was an unexplainable mixture of pleasures for all four men. The uncontrolled actions of all of the male with male sex, was creating joys of great proportions and internal excitement in all of them.

The, — who was on top, the, —who was getting fucked, the, —who was eating ass, and the, —who's ass was it, or the, —who did I just fuck, as well as the, —who just fucked me, changed quite a number of different times. Every ass, every dick, and every mouth, got its full share of pleasures and action.

Often after one of the more intensive sessions, all four men would simply lay down and re-coup for a few minutes, before once again attaching an ass or a dick that he had not yet had the opportunity to get at yet, or he had found so exciting that he just had to go get it again. The four men were experiencing more sexual actions, and inter-play, than any happy group of eight, would normally have.

Jim and Bill had both been fucked by Tom. They had of course, both been fucked by Brian again, but they had both been interested in getting fucked by Tom so that they could judge his fucking abilities, as compared to Brian's.

After about the fourth or fifth switching of positions, and after the hours had moved on, and the moon had moved across the sky, Jim reached over, placed his arm over Bill's chest and asked, "Hey guys. Would you two mind if Bill and I retreated back to the cabin and kind of spent some, oh,—some private time together back there? There's three bedrooms in the house, so use whichever one you guys want, and we'll see you both in the morning. OK? Is that OK?"

Immediately Tom exclaimed. "Yeah, Jim that is perfect! Jim you are a perfect host. It sure works for me, and I hope like hell it is OK with Brian. I really kind of love both of you guys, but since Brian is the single guy here, besides me, I was kind of hoping that things might work out to where he and I could spent the night together in each others arms, or maybe in each other's asses! Brian, everything OK with you? Can you and I sleep together tonight?"

Brian was in a complete state of shock that he even needed to answer that question.

"Oh my God Tom! Why in the hell would you even think you needed to even ask me that question? Tom, of all of the nights when I have jerked myself off, making believe my hand was your mouth, or that it was your ass, how in the hell can you even think I need to be asked? Oh thank you God!" Brian exclaimed as he looked up.

Jim and Bill both got up without saying anything further. They each smiled at each other. They took each other, hand in hand, and headed for the cabin.

As they left, hand in hand, Bill looked back toward Brian and Tom, and said, "Goodnight, guys!" And with firm bare asses hanging out, thick muscular dicks swinging side to side, each other looking at his man with a gleam in his eye and holding a firm grip to the hand he is holding, they walked on together, toward the house.

As the two entered the house, still without a word, they went to the front bedroom, turned on a small, low light lamp that was beside the bed, and they each laid down.

Still silent, Bill laid down on his back and Jim laid down on his side, up close and tight to Bill's body. Jim placed his hand on Bill's left tit. Bill submitted himself by expressively putting both of his hands up above his head, and inter-twinning his fingers. He was expressing his complete and total submission to his bed-mate. He smiled, he winked and Jim placed his lips down so gently onto Bill's right tit. Bill slightly moaned. He moved his torso to express a complete pleasure of feeling Jim's right hand on his left tit, and Jim's mouth resting on his right tit. Jim sucked on the tit slightly, he ran his tongue around in circles, loving, on the tit.

Jim's right hand fingers slightly squeezed Bill's tit. Bill moaned a very pleasant and encouraging moan, and he moved his torso so that his tit would move against the squeeze of Jim's fingers. Jim understood, and he took a more firmly placed grip. His mouth opened wider and he placed his teeth on Bill's tit. Bill moaned and brought his hands down so that he could reach around Jim's torso and give him a firm and loving hug. He pulled Jim up closer to himself! He squeezed. Jim pinched the left tit and bit the right tit. Bill squeezed Jim's waist as he moaned and groaned an un-stated happiness and acceptance.

Slowly and silently Jim repositioned himself so that his face was squarely in the middle of Bill's chest. He moved his right hand, up to grasp the back of Bill's head. He moved his left hand up to the back of Bill's neck. Bill moaned his pleasure! He looked into Jim's eyes and silently expressed his complete pleasure of submitting to his new sex buddy! Only a day ago, just a neighbor, and now, in bed together, his new sex buddy!

Bill raised his head, looked squarely into the eyes of Jim, immediately grabbed the back of Jim's head with both hands and pulled Jim's lips to his own. He pulled Jim's face up tight and gave him a very strong and a very meaningful long and strong kiss.

Jim returned the new found expression of love by returning the kiss with at least as much intensity and care. Jim and Bill were in the stages of finding a new and a very exciting style of new love. A love that was feeling so very natural and pure.

Bill hugged Jim. Jim grabbed a hold of Bill and pulled him as close to him as possible, and Jim buried his face against Bill's neck. He kissed Bill's shoulder. He moaned, but did not say a word, a very strong expression of, "Thank you for letting me be with you and love you!" Bill silently expressed the same love back, as he strongly squeezed Jim and made Jim gasp for air.

Jim removed his face from beside Bill's neck and so very slowly started letting his lips slide down the front of Bill's body. He positioned his face right between both of Bill's tits and with each hand, grabbed a tit and at the same time kissed the middle of Bill's chest. He ran his tongue around in slight circles, and then continued his trip down toward Bill's slightly hairy belly button. He licked and loved as he moved his face. As he approached Bill's stomach he allowed his tongue to enter into Bill's navel. He licked and slightly chewed on the edge of it. Bill pushed Jim's head down into his navel. He moaned another pleasure! Jim slightly rubbed Bill's sides and moved his hands down onto the top, outside, of Bill's legs.

As Jim moved his face down farther, he used his chin to move to the side, Bill's stiff hard-on! Jim moved to position himself so that he could take a small mouth full of Bill's bush hair. He so very slightly bit on the hair, and so very slightly pulled on it. Bill moaned. He approved and was actually pleading for more of the same. He was being loved by Jim and all of Jim's actions. He was in his own small heaven.

Jim took Bill's cock into his mouth. He sucked on it, and he forced as much of it down his throat as he could manage. He rolled Bill's cock around the back of his throat. Suddenly Jim realized that he was actually making love to Bill rather than just having sex with him. He knew that sex was much more active than this. This, —this warm exchange of emotions, he knew was loving, and not just sex! He too, now knew that he was also in his own small heaven!

Jim loved on Bill, and Bill knew what was happening. He deeply felt the exchange of emotions between the two. Bill returned the love, although he was the one with his dick stuffed in Jim's mouth. He felt an actual transmission of love and caring pass from himself to Jim, as he accepted the sucking that he was receiving from Jim. He intuitively could tell that Jim was doing more than just sucking some guy's cock. He was making love to it, and it was part of Bill, and one of the most private parts of Bill.

Jim pulled off of Bill's rod after quite a long, extended, period of time, and each man grabbed the other person and took him into a complete, strong, and forceful body hug.

Bill kissed Jim on the side of the neck and said, "Hon, this may not be right, but I do love you. Being with you is so much more than just the sex. Yeah, —it's been fun learning how to do the gay guy stuff, but Jim, I'm moving way beyond that. Sex is only part of what I am feeling and enjoying. I've gone way past that! Jim, I love you! Yeah, —I know, I know it's wrong for me to tell you that, but Jim, it's the honest truth. I do love you!"

"Bill I know that, and I've got to admit too, that, —yeah, —yes, —I love you too. You know Bill, when you first suggested the idea that we do something together, that really shocked me like hell, but I really think that's only because I've looked at you before and kind of wondered what it would be like to just hug you. Bill, I don't know why, but whenever I've been around you, I've always felt kind of dirty with just the wondering of what it would be like to be really close to you, or to be able to just feel you. Bill, I've been trying to convince myself ever since we were at the Cafe together, that you are just another guy, but Bill, I just have not been able to do that. Bill, —I love you too. I guess I really have ever since I originally met you and worked with you on that community committee. Hell man, guess I ought to just admit it right now! The second committee we worked on together was only because I found out you were already on the committee. If you had not been on that committee, neither would I have been. Bill, I didn't really want to do that community stuff, I only did it because I could be close to you. You know Bill, I never really fully thought it thorough. I made those moves kind of blindly and unconsciously. If I had really thought it out back then, I'd have forced myself to go the other direction since that was just being a little too close to being funny. Know what I mean? Bill, today, being funny or not, I really don't give a damn! Bill, —I love you man! What in the hell are we going to do? We each have wives. I've got kids. Bill, what in the hell are we going to do? I know now that I'm living the wrong life, but I can't change that! Bill, what in the hell are we going to do?"

"Hey Jim, we've just got to take things good and slow. Yeah, —you are right. We both have wives and you have kids too. Jim, I'm sure a lot of guys find themselves in this funny situation. We are just going to have play it real cool. You know, we can just be better and closer friends than we have been before, and hey—we'll just have to come up here to the cabin by ourselves just as often as we can work it out. I don't have kids at my house, so maybe we will be able to find some private times at my house when we know Sue will be gone for awhile. Jim, fortunately I've got the workroom out in the garage, and I'll be able to store some stuff for us out there since Sue never gets into my tools and all that stuff. We can use part of the garage as a playroom when we want to get together."

"God yeah, —I guess." Jim replied. "Bill, life is getting real funny all of a sudden. Bill, hold me. Squeeze me. I need to feel you up against me! Oh Bill, hug me tight! Bill, let's go to sleep. I want to feel your arms around me while I go to sleep. Bill, I want us to be able to go to sleep like this every night! Hug me man, I need you!"

A Boner Book

CHAPTER THIRTEEN:

Getting Up Sunday Morning

The sun rose bright and sharp, and shined directly into Bill and Jim's bedroom and slowly but very brightly woke Jim up. Laying there with his eyes only slightly opened to avoid the bright sunlight, Jim realized that he and his new love were laying in almost the same exact position that they were in when they had gone to sleep the night before. Jim quietly laid there and just smiled at Bill. As so often can happen, a sleeping person can have some unexplained feelings that they are being watched, totally silently, but none the less watched, and will then wake up. Bill did just that! He slowly opened his eyes, closed them again quickly because of the direct sunshine, and then opened them up a little more slowly as he focused on Jim's face and his smile.

"Hey buddy! Hi! Good morning!" Bill managed as he struggled to come alive.

"Hi guy! How you doing?" Jim replied.

"Horny as hell man!" Bill expressed as he grinned at Jim. "Damn it man! I guess it's because I know that once we get up out of this bed, it's over for us till we can sneak out sometime and get it on again. Shit man, I do not want to go home! Really Jim, I don't. I want you and me to just stay here and be with each other!"

"I know, I sure know that one! I kind of think you and I just might have a rough day in front of us today. You know Bill. If it was just one of us that felt that way, we'd probably be a lot more able to handle it since the other guy could just brush if off as stupid thinking, but man, since we are both feeling the same way, it is going to be rough letting the other guy just go home and each of us trying to act like nothing happened this weekend! It's not going to be easy, but it is something that we just have to do. We are just going to have to always keep our eyes open for opportunities of when we can get together and hopefully fuck and suck each other. Right?"

"Yeah right you are Jim. I'm not happy with that, but I guess that's the way it will have to be."

"OK, —before we start the day, well, I mean get up and start the day, let me run in and take a good long morning piss, and then come back in here and pump your ass one more time. OK?"

"Yeah, that's OK, but I'm going to need to take a good piss too, or you will be pushing all my piss out every time you push down on me. Come on. Let's go do a buddy piss, —outdoors! OK?"

"Oh hell yes! Yeah, —I forget we are all just guys up here right now, and we can run around bare ass naked and let our dicks fly and go piss outdoors and do all that good ole manly stuff! Yeah, —let's go water the grass!"

As they left their bedroom, Bill suggested, "Hey let's be quiet going out so we don't wake up Brian and Tom. I don't know which room they decided to use."

Jim agreed and each man quietly left the room, crossed across the living room and went out the door headed toward the pier.

As they left the house and stepped onto the porch, Jim rather quickly and excitedly said, "Oh shit! Bill look at that! Holly crap!"

"I'll be damned!" Bill replied. "Well shit man, we sure did not need to worry about waking those two up did we?"

"Hell no, I guess not!"

Bill and Jim were completely taken back by the sight that they were presented with, as they headed out. Tom and Brian were already up and at it, outdoors. Tom was stretched out, laying on the top of a rather large log, length wise. His body was resting along the length of the log with his arms slightly drooped down on each side with his hands up under his face to lay his face on, and each leg was extended down on each side of the log. On top of Tom was Brian. Well, rather on top of him, and in him. He was fucking Tom's ass as Tom laid there and rather hugged the log. Brian needed to maintain a delicate balance on top of Tom so that he did not fall sideways. He was attempting to make Tom and the log become one. He was fucking Tom so damn hard that Bill and Jim just took gasps of air each time Brian slammed down on Tom's ass. Neither man, —the one that was getting rambunctiously fucked, nor the one that was doing the fucking, knew that Bill and Jim were watching them make some of the hottest looking, and steamiest sex, that had happened so far this week-end.

"Oh shit man! Oh God, that looks hot!" Jim exclaimed. "My God Bill, can you imagine what that position must feel like to Tom with all of Brian's dick up in him? My God man, that his hot! My God Bill, it's a struggle to just get all of Brian's cock up in your ass, just laying level and relaxing! Can you imagine what in the hell it must feel like to have your legs spread that far apart and then have him ram that hunk of meat up in you? God man, I'm surprised that Tom can take it that way! Shit, Tom's ass must feel like he has got a whole fucking whale up in him right now! My God man! That is hot as hell to me! Oh Bill, I've got to get fucked like that! Oh man! I want to do that! I've got to get fucked like that!"

Bill and Jim slowly and quietly walked over toward the direction of the two fucking men and their log. As they approached somewhat closer, Tom flipped his face from the right to the left, and saw the two men standing there watching him get one hell of one rambunctious and exciting ass fucking. Tom just simply grinned and moved his lips around his mouth as if to indicate that he was really enjoying this. Brian still did not know they had an audience. His complete attention was directed to using Tom's ass for as much complete fun and pleasure as he could get from it, and nothing around him was of any importance.

Suddenly and without warning, Brian started screaming, "I'm cumin! I'm cumin! Tom, I'm cumin! Oh God man, I'm cummmmmin!"

Bill and Jim would have been able to tell what was happening, even if Brian had not made the loud verbal announcement. His body tightened up completely, and they could tell from his torso's jerking that he was letting his body do its natural release of male juices. They didn't need to hear him say a thing! They could tell, —just by watching him, —that his body was in total glory with its climax!

After his proclaimed cumin session, Brian completely collapsed down onto Tom's body. He gasped for air. Bill and Jim could hear him telling Tom, that he was, "Fucking exhausted! I'm fucking exhausted!"

Jim and Bill stood there and were each completely taken with the sights and sounds that they had just experienced. All of this type of action was so totally new and extremely exciting to them. They each felt as if they were now walking in a completely new and exciting world. They were now watching, and were involved in actions that they had never imagined before, —but actions that they now wished they had been involved in for many, many years.

"Oh God man! Oh God, that was hot!" Jim exclaimed as he stood there and stroked his own rod. "God Bill, I never imagined things could be this exciting out in the woods! Oh man that was hot!"

"Oh shit yes it was!" Jim replied as he too stood there and managed his excitement by grabbing his own dick and slamming it back and forth as if he was trying to abuse himself with it. "Shit man! I have never seen anything like that! God Bill, that was hot as hell! Oh shit man, I am so damn glad we came out when we did! Man that is something I never imagined before. Bill, a man and a woman just can not have sex that hot! There is no way a man and a woman can do it like that! Yeah, some gal could lay down on a log like that, but man, no way in hell would it turn out that damn hot! No woman could take it up in the ass that damn rough! Oh Bill, please fuck me like that! I've got to get fucked that way! Oh man, I've got to feel that! I want to see what that feels like!"

Brian finally heard the other two men as he recomposed himself. He looked over toward them and grinned. "I guess I kind of screamed when I came didn't I? Did I wake you guys up?"

Jim looked at Brian, still re-cooping, laying along the top of Tom's stretched out body, and replied, "Oh no man! No, no! We've been standing here for probably five or six minutes watching you go for that ass. God you fucked his ass! My God man, what a fucking hot session that was! They don't make pornos any hotter than that was! Fuck man that was good!"

"Man, I hope it was OK that I screamed out like that! I knew I was doing that! I have wanted to scream that out loud, outdoors when I cum for years. I thought maybe this morning was my best chance of doing it. There's nobody else except us four close around here, —are there? Shit I hope not anyway! If there are, I'm sure they now know that I just shot one hell of a big wad!"

"No, I don't think anybody else is around. Unless they hiked in during the night. If so, let's just hope they are hot and hunky gay guys." Jim told Brian. "Tom saw us here a minute or so just before you let it all fly. Wish you could have seen his face while you were making babies in his ass. Man, when you let out that first scream, I think Tom thought some fucking hand grenade was going to blow up in his ass! I wish you could have seen his face. No way in hell to explain what it looked like, but I do think he was wondering just how safe his ass was right then. God man, I have never seen, well yeah I guess that's obvious, but I have never seen that much excitement in somebody having sex. God that was fucking hot! I don't know who is going to do it, but I need to get my ass fucked like that!"

"Well, I would say that since poor ole Tom is still trying to find out if he is even still alive after that one or not, and I am completely whipped, as you can see from my prone position yet on top of poor Tom, I would say that the best person available right now would be Bill. And besides from the strength of that rod he is supporting out in front of him right now, I'd say that one looks like it sure as the hell could feel pretty damn good going up in you, don't you think Jim?"

Jim and Bill were still feeling real sexy from watching the actions that had just taken place and each of them stood there, rather watching Brian and Tom get up from their position on the log, and both men were unconsciously stoking and pulling on their cocks and Bill had unconsciously discovered that pinching his own tit was another good feeling at a time like this!

Brian and Tom had used one of the blankets from down on the dock as some soft protection from the rough log surface, and Tom did suggest that they use that rug too. He told them how in the middle of the night, when the log action originally got started, they were not using a rug, and they quickly decided that if they were going to do that, Tom definitely needed something between him and the old log.

Jim took the position that Tom had just removed himself from, and laid down along the log with his legs down on each side. Even this simple position of laying on top of this log, totally naked, bare ass up in the air, was exciting to Jim. The feel of having something that shape and that firm under him made his body react, and even though there were no orifices to use, Jim did hump the log a couple of times after he initially laid down on it.

Bill used some of the grease that Tom and Brian had brought up from the dock with them, and he not only greased up his cock, but he also used that action to rather play with himself enough to where Brian saw what was happening and offered to help smear the grease around and to make sure all parts top and bottom of Bill's cock were well coated.

Bill swung his leg over the log and positioned himself above Jim. He scooted himself forward and got his rod in position to ram his buddy Jim when they were both ready!

"Hey guy! You ready for this?" Bill asked of Jim.

"Oh hell yes I am man! Yes I am! Fuck me and my ass like Brian fucked Tom's ass. Fuck me baby!"

Bill raised up his mid section, aimed his rod, found Jim's asshole and went in, —quickly and forcefully, he went in! All the way in!

Jim let out a scream, and then very quickly a, "Yes! Oh yes! Oh God yes! Oh yeah fuck me baby! Fuck me hard! Oh God man, what a fucking feeling this is! Oh man I would have never thought to get fucked this way! Oh man this is the way to get your ass fucked! Man this is fucking great! Oh God, I'm so glad we saw you guys doing this! Oh this is great!"

Bill used Jim's ass just about as roughly as Brian had done to Tom, and then he too suddenly started yelling, "I'm cumin! I'm cumin man, —I'm cummmmin! Oh God man, oh man, I just shot it all!"

After a moment of regrouping and getting some air, Bill continued, "Oh man, that felt great! Oh shit man, that makes your ass feel so damn tight. Shit, it sure did not take me long to cum! You OK Jim?"

"Yeah I'm OK, how you doing? You OK?"

"Yeah, I'm OK, —exhausted, but OK. Hey Hon. Brian is standing here watching me ram you, and he's got an enormous hard on again, that he is standing there rubbing. I kind of think he might like to mount you. You want Brian to fuck you before you get up, and while you're still hugging this log?"

"Oh hell yes I do! Fuck yes! Hell yeah man! I am taking advantage of every fucking I can get or give while I can. Hell yes! Tell him to get over here and get on me! Tell him to fuck me with that damn pole of his!"

Bill looked at Brian as if to say, "OK get ready," and he then pulled out of Jim and Brian immediately mounted Jim as if he was a horse. He placed his hands up by Jim's shoulders on the log, he lifted his right leg, jumped and landed right on Jim's back just as if he was landing on the back of some big strong horse. Brian slightly raised himself up, he aimed and he slammed his big rod down into Jim's ass.

"Oh my God! Oh shit!" Jim did scream. "Oh shit man, how many cocks did he just slam up in me? Oh my asshole! Oh my God, —my ass! Oh shit Brian you have such a fucking big cock! Oh Brian, lay there and just push down in me and let me get used to it. Oh fuck! What a fucking experience. Men, this is great! Oh man I love to be fucked! I never knew that, until this week-end, but man I sure as the hell know it now! I love it! Oh my God my ass is full!"

Brian rested on top of Jim for a moment or two until he knew Jim was really ready to get fucked like he had just seen Tom get fucked. "You ready man? You want a good fucking, right?"

"Oh fuck, oh shit!" Jim replied. "Oh man, I don't know if I can take it like Tom did with you having this much fucking dick. Brian, I feel like you are using every little bit of me already. Brian, I'm not sure if I can really get fucked by you like that!"

"Well, tell you what!" Brian said. "I know damn well that if we don't take it to your outer limit, then you are always going to wonder if maybe you could have taken just a little more, so what I want to do is start off kind of slow and gentle, and when I hit the point where you need to yell "Uncle," I promise to stop. OK? Game for that Jim?"

"Yeah, —I guess." Jim answered. "Yeah, I know I want it, so I guess what you said is OK. Yeah Brian, but I don't know how much I can take, OK?"

Brian uttered a low "OK" and then started on Jim's ass in a nice, slow and gentle manner. As Jim laid there, hugging the tree log, Brian listened for any negative remarks or comments and when he heard none, he stepped up his speed, his force, and his depth down into the lower sections of Jim's ass.

"You doing OK?" Brian asked.

"Yeah, yeah I'm OK." Jim replied.

"OK, I'm going to increase it some." Brian replied.

"OK."

Brian and Jim had this interchange probably four or five times before Brian was letting Jim have it in the ass just as roughly as he had fed it to Tom earlier. One minute, two minutes, three minutes and Brian was headed into the fourth minute of his fast and furious fucking when all of a sudden he let out a yell, "Jim, Jim, —I'm going to cum! I'm about to cum! Jim you want it up in the ass? Jim, tell me if you want it in the ass or on your back and hurry up, I'm about to cum!"

"In my ass and pound me! Fuck me and load me! Make me feel it hit up in me! Cum in my ass!"

"I'm cummmmmin! I'm cummmmin!! Brian yelled out. "Jim your ass is getting my juicy cum, man! Oh shit man! I did not think I'd be doing that after how I loaded Tom up! Shit man! I really don't remember any other time that I shot that much twice in such a short time! Man,—I am fucking exhausted!"

Still laying there with Brian re-cooping on his back, and thoroughly up in his butt, Jim kind of yelled, "Hey, Brian, you need to get off of me, I've got to piss! Brian, let me up!"

"Hey hold it man!" Brian immediately yelled as he quickly started to climb off of Jim. "Hold it man! Don't let it go yet! I want you to pee on me! Come on Jim, spray me! Pee on me!"

Brian immediately sank down on his knees and grabbed a hold of Jim's sides. Brian leaned forward so that when Jim started to pee, it would hit him in the face!"

Jim was kind of shocked and stunned, but Bill looked at Jim with a big grin on his face, smiled, and remembered a very recent fun time that he and Jim had shared in the shower together.

Tom just said, "Hey good! Great man!"

As Jim started to let his urine flow, Tom immediately rushed over beside Jim, and he too started pissing, and aiming it right onto Brian.

"Hey Bill!" Tom yelled to Bill. "Get over here and let Brian have it! We've got a guy here that likes to feel good warm piss on him, and we need to help him out! Get over here and pee!"

Still somewhat surprised, but pleased, as to what was happening, Bill did come over and after only just a moment or two, he too started peeing and he too aimed it directly at Brian. He did not immediately aim for Brian's face, but Brian moved himself so that Bill's warm golden piss would hit him right in the forehead.

"Oh shit man!" Jim said as he looked over at Bill, secretly grinned and then said, "It sure does look like Brian wants it."

Bill and Jim shared a rather private moment between themselves about their prior drinking session, that neither felt the necessity of expounding on.

Brian responded with a, "Yeah! Yes I do! I love to have hot looking guys pee on me! It is great! I can't believe it! Three guys peeing on me all at once! Man, this is great!"

All three men finally finished their peeing, and Brian thanked each and every one of them for a great treat!

"I knew I wanted that, but I just knew I had to be patient until the time was right. I knew it'd be OK with Tom. He pissed on me last night. But I was kind of afraid that if I just asked you two for it, then you two guys might not be too keen to doing it. Hey, —it worked out great this way! OK, now I'm going to go jump in the lake and kind of wash it off. Love to feel it hit me and kind of taste it when it is happening, but for some funny reason, I'm usually ready right away to rinse off. Hey, anybody gonna join me in the water?"

"Yeah, I will!" Jim answered.

"Yeah, I will!" Bill answered also.

"Don't leave me out!" Tom replied.

All four men headed for the dock, and very shortly there were four splashes as all four men dived in.

As they were enjoying the early morning swim, and of course for Brian the rinse off, Bill and Jim had a chance to find out and rather get caught up, on just how Brian and Tom had spend the night, following the four way actions that had happened, on the dock, when all four of the men took advantage of each other and everybody, and everything.

Jim asked, "Hey Tom, Brian said that you pissed on him last night. When did that happen?"

"Oh, that was down here on the dock. We've been up all night!" Tom explained. "Yeah, we never went to bed. We haven't even been up to the cabin since all of us came down to the dock last night."

"What! You guys never went to bed?" Jim asked

"Yeah, I mean, no! Hell, —what I mean is, —we never went to bed. I have known, well anyway have heard about Brian's big rod for a long time now, although I was never really sure of just who they were talking about, and once I found out it was him, I sure as the hell was not going to waste all of last night with just sleeping beside it. If it had been stuck up in me, then I might have gone to sleep, but shit man, he has a permanent hard-on and last night I was going to take advantage of it! We fucked! Well, let's say he fucked me for most of the night! We fucked first down here on the dock. Then we decided that we needed a change of environment, so we went over there, right close to the water edge. Then after we did some fucking over there, then I decided that I wanted to know what it was like to get fucked under water, so we got in the lake. We kind of took it pretty slow there because I've been told that you should never get fucked when you ass is under water because that could force too much water up in your ass and cause problems. But I guess I just never really thought that could happen. I douche my ass with a lot, and I do mean a lot of water right out of a shower hose, so I guess I was pretty confident that everything would be OK. So anyway, we talked about it and I still decided I wanted to do it. It felt good, and I'm glad we did. Then after that, I of course, wanted to see if he could fuck my mouth while under water, so then we did that! That is so much fun! You really have to hold your breath and suck on him at the same time. If you forget to hold your breath, all of a sudden you have more stuff to deal with than just a dick in your mouth. Anyway, then he had me fuck his mouth while he was under water. Well, —then, yeah, —that's when we decided to come up here and find some of nature's stuff that we could play with a little."

"Nature's stuff? What do you mean nature's stuff?" Bill asked.

"Little whips. Little branches that we could kind of whip each other with. I know, —weird stuff, but while talking about doing weird stuff, we both found out that we each like to kind of get whipped, as long as it is from some hot guy. We admitted that unless it is from some guy, we have no interest in it, but as long it is being swung by some guy, then it is hot! So, anyway we found a couple of branches that ended up feeling damn good. I did find out, —hate to admit it though, —that Brian can take a lot more pain and whipping back there than I can. I had hit my limit, and he begged and begged for me to keep it up and he kept yelling, 'Harder, Harder'. Fact is, once, I looked up at the cabin to see if any lights had come on. He was really begging for it. If you look, I'll bet you will see some whip marks on his ass!"

Jim and Bill asked Brian to turn around so they could see his ass.

"Well, I'll be damned! You do have whip marks back there!" Bill exclaimed!

"Shit man, doesn't that hurt to be whipped with a stick like that?"

Brian grinned, and replied. "Yeah, yeah it does, but that's why I like it! For some reason, some people like certain kinds of pain, and getting paddled or whipped is mine, as long as it's from some hot looking guy! Why, I don't know, but as long as it's some hot guy that's whipping me, I like it! And as Tom will agree, I like it strong and rough! Tom found that out last night!"

Tom then continued his juicy description of what had happened the night before. "So anyway, after we decided that we needed to find something different to do, we realized that that log that we were using might be fun. So we started fucking there, and then you guys came out! Well, anyway, after we had baptized that log about six or eight times, at least!"

"Uhh, Tom, Mr. Tom Sir!" Brian entered. "Uhhhhh Mr. Tom you rather failed to explain of just why we went to the log. It wasn't originally for fucking now was it? Tom, why did we go over to the log?"

"OK, OK!" Tom answered. "Right. Fucking was not the original reason for going over to the log. I wanted Brian's ass spread out good and open so I could run my face up in there, as far as I could! I just figured that if he had his legs hanging down on each side of the log, then his ass would be real open and exposed, and then I would be able to get up in there good and close!"

"Well, did you?" Jim asked. "Did that work?"

"Oh yes, yes it did! Brian answered. "It worked like it worked when we were in the water, and when we were on the edge of the water, and when we were on the dock. Hey, he didn't need my ass spread across that log to get to it! He kind of forgot to tell you when he describing last night, that it was more like fuck me a little, then eat my ass out a lot! I'm sure not complaining, but he did kind of forget to tell you that he ate more air out of my ass last night than he did from normal breathing. Didn't you, —Mr. Tom?"

"OK, OK! I'll admit it Brian, I'll admit it! We tried to figure out some way where I could have my face stuck in his ass, and his dick up in my ass at the same time, and it just did not work! We tried, but it didn't work. So he'd fuck me, then I'd eat him out! That worked pretty good!"

"OK men, there had to be some fucking and some ass eating, but nobody's mentioned any cock sucking yet! Did you guys forget to do that since you both seemed to be so busy with asses?"

"Oh hell no!" Tom replied. "Every time the other one of us had our mouth open, but not saying anything, that was a good reason to stick your dick in it! Oh no! Sucking, definitely was not forgotten! With as much sucking that went on last night, we could have gone through a full case of lolly pops!"

"Shit man!" Jim said as he looked at Bill. "Sounds like those two had one hell of a night wile we slept, don't it? Damn, sounds like you two kinda hit it off pretty well together, didn't you?"

As Tom put his arm around Brian's neck, he answered. "You know guys, we talked about that some last night too. Yeah, —especially me since I've now found out about the railroad car of his, and thanks to you two guys, we now both think there just might be some future for the two of us. Yeah, we know there are a lot of things that need to be talked about, and worked out, but we sure are gonna try! Thanks for helping us finally get together!"

As Jim listened to Tom talk about their new relationship, he put his arm around Bill's neck and allowed one tear to slide down his cheek.

Tom saw it! "Jim, you alright? Jim, did I say something wrong?"

"No Tom, you sure did not! It's just what you did say though. Tom, Bill and I have discovered a new relationship this weekend too, and we have already admitted to each other that we wish we could become partners, but you know things are a little different for us. Listen guys, if you mean something to each other, go for it and make it work! Do everything you can for each other!"

As Jim finished that statement of encouragement, Bill grabbed him, spun him around, and gave him a tremendous great big bear hug and a kiss!

The emotions of the moment were too much for Brian, and he likewise grabbed Tom, spun him around and gave him a great big bear hug, and a kiss!

Both couples stood there for more than just a few minutes and hugged their respective man. Finally, Jim and Bill started to release each other and as they separated, so did Tom and Brian. All four men had tears in their eyes! Jim looked at Bill and wiped away a tear as Bill did the same to Jim. They each grinned at each other and Jim said, "We'll work it out someway honey, some way!"

Tom looked at Brian, pulled him even closer and wiped a tear from each eye. Brian returned the favor.

Tom looked at Brian and said, "Oh thank God we finally, finally know each other. Babe, we have a good chance, we can do it! I know we can!"

Brian grabbed Tom and while giving him another big hug, he answered, "Yes Hon, —yes we can! Yes, I know we can do it! We will do it!"

Then turning toward Bill and Jim, Brian once again said, "Thank you men, thank you! Because of you two, Tom and I are now headed for a new life! I just know we are! Thank you!"

That started a four man hug and each man then hugged each other, —man to man, —individually. Bare skin to bare skin, each man expressed his love and genuine concern for each other man.

Jim looked at Brian and simply said, "You are welcome. You are very welcome. I'm not just so sure of what Bill and I did, but if you think we did something, so be it! Now guys, just make the best of it! Do whatever you can for your man!"

Bill stood there with his arm sound Jim and said, "Men, if we really did help you two get together, then this week-end ended up even better than I thought! And me, finally getting to know my man, and my real self, has already been a pretty good thing for me! All I ask of you two is, stay friends with us. We've got some rocky days ahead of us, and I just know that if we can count on you two as some real solid friends, then somehow, we will make it too! Right now, I'm just not too sure of how, but we will do it! I'm sure!"

Jim squeezed Bill's waist, pulled him up closer and said, "Bill I stand here in whole, bare assed and all, and if you will let me, I will be yours, and together, somehow we will make it work! It will, —I know it will!"

Once again, all four men met together in one very big group hug, and silently they each knew, that all four lives had changed during this very, special, unusual, and very different kind of a week-end.

ABOUT THE AUTHOR

Wade Wright

Wade Wright is a semi-retired father of two daughters and four grandchildren. Transplanted many years ago from the state of Ohio, to the Southwest, now living alone, —well with the exception of his Min Pin puppy, which has been his sole love for the past eight years! Enjoyed two gentlemen partnerships that each ended <u>way</u> before they were suppose to.

Wade Wright is also the author of ***Apartment 117***, available from Amazon.com, TheNazcaPlainsCorp.com or your local bookstore.

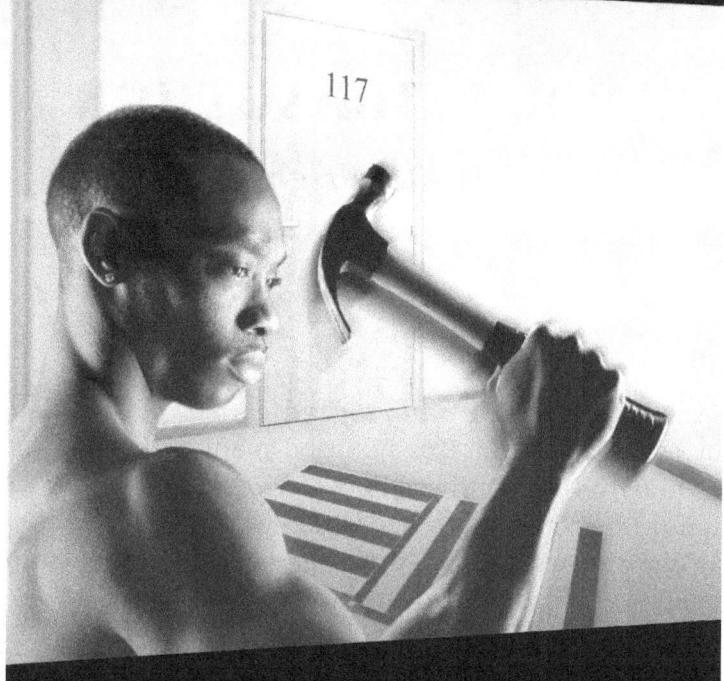

APARTMENT 117

a novel by
WADE WRIGHT

A BONER BOOK

www.ingramcontent.com/pod-product-compliance
Lightning Source LLC
Chambersburg PA
CBHW051126260626
47170CB00005B/1680